Shena Mackay was born in Edinburgh in 1944, and grew up in London and Kent. She admits to have 'been writing ever since I could lift a pen'; her first two stories were written when she was nineteen, and the following three when she was in her early twenties. Her work includes: *Toddler on the Run* and *Dust Falls on Eugene Schlumberger* (1964), *Music Upstairs* (1965), *Old Crow* (1967), *An Advent Calendar* (1971), *Babies in Rhinestones* (1983), *A Bowl Of Cherries* (1984) and *Redhill Rococo* (1986). She writes poetry and has also written a play – *Nurse Macater* – for the National Theatre.

Also by Shena Mackay in Abacus:

BABIES IN RHINESTONES

A BOWL OF CHERRIES

REDHILL ROCOCO

Dreams of Dead Women's Handbags

Shena Mackay

An *Abacus* Book

First published in Great Britain by William Heinemann 1987
This edition published by Abacus 1989
Reprinted 1992

'The Thirty-first' October first appeared in
Woman's Journal in October 1986

A CIP catalogue record for this book
is available from the British Library.

ISBN 0 349 10037 3

Printed in England by Clays Ltd, St Ives plc

Abacus
A Division of
Little, Brown and Company (UK) Limited
165 Great Dover Street
London SE1 4YA

To Elsa

Contents

Electric-Blue Damsels

YOU see them in the Underground with their schoolbooks and across the counters of shops and waiting on tables in restaurants, slinging burgers and pushing brooms; girls and boys in whom an exotic cocktail of genes has been shaken into a startling and ephemeral beauty: birds of paradise nesting in garbage, or captive tropical fish shimmering in the gloomy backrooms of dank pet shops.

At almost sixteen Fayette Gordon was not weaving blossoms in her hair, or diving for pearls in a green translucent ocean; she was a pupil at a comprehensive school, and in these summer evenings, which should have been heavy with the scents of frangipani and mimosa instead of those of melting tarmac and diesel fumes, she worked in a chip shop with the traffic's surf pounding on the pavement's crumbling shore. Her ancestry and origins were mysterious to everybody, except perhaps her grandmother with whom she lived, whose clenched teeth behind purple lips suggested the loss of a short-stemmed pipe. Fayette was breathtaking; at least her year-tutor Maurice Barlow always caught his rather pipe-smelling breath on catching sight of her unexpectedly in the corridor or on the tennis court. At once his teeth felt scummy and he put away the pipe which convention, if increasingly begrudgingly, allowed him; a round red burn on his fuzzy thigh and a singed pocket testified to his haste on one occasion; her teeth, her blouse, her socks were so white.

It had been the worst sort of weather, as so often, for exams; the sort of weather which inspired unironic comments on 'flaming June', when swotting sweating adolescents in rolled-up shirt-sleeves dreamed of sea and sand and returned from Sundays at the coast with the bruised purple fruit of love-bites on their necks. Fayette's neck was unblemished and of course she did not sweat, except for a once-glimpsed row of tiny seed pearls beading her upper lip after a strenuous mixed doubles one lunch hour; her exam papers, although less than brilliant, would bear no unseemly smudges; she wore invisible white gloves. Maurice Barlow thought of white communion dresses, parasols and jalousies, iron lace balconies, guavas and jacaranda. Thin silver bangles rolled up and down her cinnamon-coloured wrist as she wrote, and if he was invigilating he listened for the little clink of silver on wood and agonized if there was a long silence. Her hair, he had decided, was cinnamon too, the soft pale colour of the most delicious Edinburgh rock, that he would never taste.

As he sat at his kitchen table with the back door open, writing reports on school-leavers, the radio throbbed out 'Summer in the City'. He took a sheet of paper and attempted to compose a reference. Fayette, he wrote, is Fayette Fayette Fayette Fayette. He crumpled it and threw it in the bin and went out into the back yard. He pulled up a few tufts of groundsel that grew beside the gate and found himself ambling down the pavement. As he was out, he thought, he might as well buy himself some supper. The pockets of his creased Terylene trousers were weighed down with loose change, the key to the stockroom cupboard, a confiscated knife, a dried-out Tipp-Ex and other schoolmasterly impedimenta. The stain of a felt-tipped pen on the breast pocket of his shirt gave his heart a wounded look. She stood in front of the vats of boiling oil, leaning on the counter, brooding into the summer evening.

'Ah, Fayette. Business slack, I see.' Was in fact delighted to see.

'Be busy later when the pubs close.'

He loved it when his pupils greeted him by name in the pub, except that most of them, he knew, were under age. They bought his silence in halves of lager. Good old Maurice. Pupils came and went but Maurice was always one of the lads. He watched Fayette dunk a basket of raw chips into the oil and wished that they would take for ever to cook and suppressed a desire to lock the door so that he and she might stay pickled in time like those eggs in a jar on the counter. The oil sizzled and spat while the closing music of 'EastEnders' was strained through the bead curtain behind which the proprietor and his family were watching television.

'Isn't that rather tactless?'

Maurice pointed to a tank of tropical fish, rosy and neon tetras brushing their fins against the plaster mermaid who reclined in the emerald green gravel combing her hair, in full view of their North Sea cousins dressed in overcoats of knobbly batter. Fayette did not answer.

'I wish you'd reconsider staying on for A levels.'

Fayette disturbed a flock of butterflies of coloured ribbon as she shook the last eleven years of her short life from her cinnamon-coloured hair.

'No way. I've had enough of school. I can't wait to leave.'

His eyes bulged cold and hard as the pickled eggs as she doused his chips in vinegar, smarting with salt at her dismissal of him and their years together.

'I think you're making a grave mistake, and one that, believe you me, you'll live to regret.'

He tapped the fish tank in emphasis.

'Believe you me,' mocked Fayette. 'Don't do that, it frightens the fish.'

'Fat lot you care.'

*

True to her word Fayette left school without an expression of regret. Maurice could remember the days when tearful girls had queued outside the staffroom door clutching damp autograph books and farewell gifts, but that had been before everything was so uncertain, before teachers were fallible and world leaders exposed as murderous liars and frauds; when girls like Fayette could step out into a secure and radiant future of physiotherapy and nursing, and teaching and secretarial posts, and then babies in coach-built prams. Fayette had announced her own plans to the careers master: she had decided to be rich and famous. Her education had ended in four minutes of ecstasy for Maurice at the leavers' disco.

'I never realized this record was so long,' she remarked as they danced.

He sat gloomily in the pub afterwards with a group of his colleagues, his Palm Beach party shirt exhibiting salty circles of drying sweat, nursing a tepid beer and dreaming of a Caribbean of the heart where he and Fayette could dance forever, of a room with a frilly iron balcony looking out over the wide Sargasso Sea. Or Fayetteville, Arkansas.

'Cheer up, Maurice. School's out for summer. Made any plans for going away yet?'

'I was thinking of the Caribbean . . .'

'On your salary? A likely tale.'

'Room for a little one? Budge up, you guys.'

Sally Molloy swung her large tanned knees under the table, so that Maurice's and her thighs sighed against each other, nudging memories of gruelling sessions of dry-skiing in East Grinstead. He had conducted a desultory affair with her over the years; he supposed he ought to ask her to marry him, she wasn't getting any younger, but something always happened to prevent him from popping the question; one of them got hiccups or cramp or the toast caught fire. He feared now that she was about to suggest a take-away, so while Patsy Armstrong, who taught social studies, engaged her in a discussion of the relative merits of the graffiti in the girls' and the boys' loos, and they laid contingency plans for the next term's half-day strikes, he stepped over Sally's designer trainers, and slipped into the night, hardly able to believe that the summer stretched before him without a prospect in sight of a cycling holiday in Holland, pot-holing in the Peak District, or following in the footsteps of St Paul; three unappetizing carrots which had been dangled in front of him earlier in the year.

He had managed also to decline, by the inspired invention of a crop of verrucas, an invitation to stay with his married sister and her four small children and enjoy their new swimming pool. His refusal had been accepted with alacrity. Uncle Maurice was whistling, albeit a melancholy tune, as he set out early with his swimming trunks in a neat towelling Swiss roll under his arm for the local pool. The company of the school rat, who was with him for the holiday, was all that he desired or found congenial in his bereft state. Fayette had given up her job in the chippie on the day that she had left school. It was to buy food for this rat, whose name, coincidentally, was Maurice too, that he entered the pet shop with his hair still wet, cleaner and red-eyed from the chlorine. His heart stopped, and stumbled on its way again.

'So this is where the rich and famous hang out.'

'Hello, Maurice.'

'What are you doing here?'

'I work here, don't I?'

'Do you?'

She was all in white; a white T-shirt under white dungarees rolled to show the delicate bones of cinnamon ankles above white plimsolls, a smudge of sawdust delineating one cheek-bone, and a small net sticking out of her chest pocket. Fish tanks glimmered like televisions with the sound turned down in the gloom of the back room. A man in a brown overall was serving a customer with biltong, or knotted strips of hide for dogs to chew. Maurice went into the back room; Fayette followed.

'Small cod and chips, open, salt and vinegar, please,' he said, then stopped. It was like walking into a gallery and being stunned by wonderful paintings by an artist whose work he had never encountered before, or entering a cave of moving jewels, rubies, emeralds, topaz, diamonds and sapphires on black velvet; like looking into Chapman's Homer. He dismissed from his mind any comparisons between keeping birds in cages and fish in aquaria.

'What are those?'

'Electric-blue damsels.'

In a flash of sapphire Maurice saw how he could get his heart's desire. They were the deepest, glowing, electric blue; slender and swift in the water.

'*Abudefduf uniocellata*,' said Fayette.

'What?'

'Formerly known as *Pomacentrus caeruleus*.'

Was this the girl who couldn't tell hake from huss?

He stood entranced in front of a tank of sea-horses twining their prehensile tails around thin poles rising from coral fans; with their equine heads and long sensitive snouts they were as ancient and mysterious as fragments of sculpture found after centuries in the ocean among starfish and the waving fronds of anemones. The only sea-horses Maurice had seen hitherto had been dry and faded curiosities in the Shell Shop in Manette Street, across from Foyles. These were moist and living, magic and mythological, undulating and grazing the water.

'*Hippocampus kuda*. Did you know that they are unique in the animal kingdom in that the male becomes pregnant and bears the young?'

'No!' Maurice was enchanted at having become the pupil.

'He incubates the eggs placed there by the female for four to five weeks in a special pouch and hundreds of perfect tiny sea-horses hatch out. Can you imagine? I can't wait to see that!'

Her eyes were shining at the thought; an enthusiastic hand fluttered a moment on his sleeve. He caught sight of his reflection in the side of a tank of black mollies in viridian weed, an albino rat displaying long teeth in an ecstatic smile, and remembered the purpose of his visit.

'Are you an arachniphobe, Maurice?'

'I don't think so. Why?'

She directed his gaze to a tarantula, but the sight that stayed with him was a pretty speckled eel curvetting upwards through the rocky water to nibble from Fayette's fingers.

His brain turned to coral: emperor and clown, harlequins, rainbows, unicorns, angels and devils, queens, jewels, damsels, glowlights, butterflies, cardinals, swordfish, surgeons, anemones, starfish, sea-horses, dancing shrimps, golden rams and silver sharks, flying foxes, albino tigers, lyretails, parrots and corals; freshwater and marine tropicals from the Indian Ocean and the Pacific swam through its branches. He took out a stack of library books. He joined the local Aquarist Society. He had to make frequent visits to the pet shop to be initiated into the mysteries of aeration and filtration, heating and lighting, salinity, and ultraviolet sterilization, ozonizing, feeding, bacteria and parasites. On one glorious evening Fayette allowed him to pick her up in his Morris Minor and drive her to an Aquarist meeting in the upper room of the library, but as there were no fish present she was bored and fidgeted and watched the clock, as in a dull lesson at school, watched covertly by the flock of old goats who, until then, Maurice had considered a pleasant bunch of chaps.

The summer holiday was almost over. Maurice wondered how he would find the time to go back to school. He went into the pet shop intent on persuading Fayette to come with him to the aquarium at the zoo, and thereafter perhaps to Brighton, to all the aquariums in the country, in far-flung cities where they would have to spend the night.

'She's not here.'

'When will she be back?'

'She won't. She's gone.'

'Gone?'

He could have wrenched the tanks from the wall, screaming in splinters of glass and the gush of water and floundering fish, dying jewels drowning in air. But only for a second; he wouldn't hurt a fish.

'I only came in for some Daphnia.'

'Of course.'

He walked out of the shop, drowning in air.

One afternoon he encountered Fayette's grandmother in a tobacconist's but she did not remember him from the one parents' evening she had attended, in Fayette's first term, when she had been a shy and heartbreaking twelve-year-old, and he could not bring himself to enquire after his former pupil. He had had to tell his disappointed fellow-Aquarists that Fayette would not be joining them again. It was after one of their meetings as he was walking home through an evening made unbearable by night-scented stocks and nicotiana mingling with the smell of diesel and chips that he saw a poster attached to the wall of a cellar wine bar, advertising live music by the Electric-Blue Damsels. He descended the steps and swam through the rocky interior where young people clung like limpets to the recesses in the walls. Now he did not want to be hailed by any pupils or ex-pupils; good old Maurice no more, he shunned the company of all but the rat, his fish and his fellow-Aquarists.

The Electric-Blue Damsels were bad by any standards. The sound system was appalling. Dominating the all-female quintet was Fayette, now leaping to pound incompetently on a synthesizer, now screeching into a hand-held mike which splattered her voice on the damp cellar walls that threw it back in echoes through the cave. The audience loved them. Her cinnamon hair was a shock of electric blue and the long bare legs under the tiny vinyl skirt ended in blue shoes with spiked heels that could tear a man's heart out, sharp as the weapon of the surgeon-fish, that has a retractable scalpel at the base of its tail. As he stumbled out he remembered that electric-blue damsels are sometimes known as blue devils.

When he did not appear on the first day of term, Sally Molloy and Patsy Armstrong went to his house after school. There was no reply to their knocking so they went round to the back. A pond had been set into the yard, almost filling it; the tragic overbred face of a bubble-eyed goldfish mouthed at the surface as they picked their way past the edge, making them gasp. The back door was open. They couldn't believe what they saw: the kitchen had liquefied. At first they thought it had flooded, then they saw that an enormous tank had been sunk into the floor. A Japanese bridge spanned its length, rising over the floating weeds and waterlilies, and at its centre stood Maurice scattering meal and watercress to a circle of the most enormous, most beautiful, metallic fish they had ever seen, phosphorescent gold and silver, monochromatic, pure white, black with reflections of scarlet or yellow, splashes of colour like ideographs and sunsets, a blazing red triangle on a snow-white head.

'Hi,' said Sally at last.

'Hi-utsuri,' Maurice replied.

'What?'

He blinked, staring at them, and did not explain. He wondered for a moment who they were.

'Did you want something? I'm very busy.'

'We just wondered if you were all right, as you didn't show up at school,' said Patsy. The woman who had once been his lover was speechless with affront, then she noticed something helping himself to what looked like a nut rissole on the bridge. 'That rat's school property, you know.'

'I wouldn't play Emil Jannings to her Marlene Dietrich.'

'What on earth are you on about?'

'*The Blue Angel.*'

They were none the wiser.

At the end of the bridge, in the front room, they could see the glitter of small fish in glass tanks.

'Did you get planning permission for this?'

He did not answer. The circle of koi fanned out and scattered like fragments in a giant kaleidoscope.

'Wouldn't they make wonderful dresses?' cried Sally. 'For

"Come Dancing". Did you sew on all the sequins yourself?'

He took a threatening step towards her as Patsy was adding, 'Or curtain fabric. Gorgeous!'

'There's only one new girl in your form,' said Sally as she retreated. 'Scarlett MacNamara.'

The combination of the exotic and the Celtic was suggestive of the name that caused him pain.

'What's she like?'

'Dark. Pretty. Very shy.'

He turned to watch his koi.

'I think I should tell you,' said Sally, 'that Patsy and I are leaving at the end of term. We're setting up an aromatherapy centre.'

'Good.'

They left Maurice standing on his Japanese bridge, staring out over the water like a man who was waiting for someone to come home.

The Most Beautiful Dress in the World

THERE are houses which exhale unhappiness. The honesty rattling its shabby discs and dominating the weedy flower bed, the carelessly rinsed bottle still veiled in milk on the step from which a tile is missing, the crisp bag, sequinned with dew-drops, which will not rot and will not be removed, clinging to the straggly hedge, are as much manifestations of the misery within as are the grey neglected nets, respectability's ghosts, clouding the windows like ectoplasmic emanations of despair.

The woman in the back garden of such a house, although with her uncombed hair falling on to the shoulders of an old pink dressing gown belted with a twisted striped tie, she looked very much in keeping with her habitat, was not, that morning, unhappy. She was lifting a mass of honeysuckle that sprawled over the grass, trying to disengage thc brittle red stems without breaking them and winding them through the almost fragile zigzags of trellis that topped the fence. The bed beneath the honeysuckle had been a herb garden and its last survivors trapping and trapped by the serpentine stems with their little ophidian heads of furled leaves, released the scent of chives. Harriet's movements were slow, with the hesitancy of one weakened by a series of blows and wounds both delivered and self-inflicted, but now, although the healing sun bathing her dressing gown and the smell of the chives on her hands could provoke weak invalidish tears, she felt convalescent, as if she had taken her first shaky steps from an asylum gate, leaving pills and bottles in a locked cabinet in a dark corridor behind her.

Other people's gardens were refulgent with sunflowers, and dahlias riddled with earwigs; the glutted trugs of Surrey bulged with late and woody runner beans. Harriet had found, at dawn, a green and yellow striped torpedo on her own step with so hard a carapace that she knew in advance how the breadknife would break as she tried to cut it and the blade would remain embedded in its shiny shell. The early October sunshine had an elegiac quality that reminded her of the slow movement of a cello concerto, still golden but foretelling full-blown autumn melancholy, the tomatoes that would never ripen, the last yellow fluted flower of the barren marrow, the falling of the leaves. The narrow lapis lazuli bracelet that rolled up and down her wrist as she worked had lost some of its stones. She had worn it for so many years that she had ceased to see it but on the rare occasions on which it had been lost, caught in a sleeve or sloughed into a shopping bag, she had been aware at once of its absence circling her arm like a bangle of air. Her daughter had played with it as a baby, had cut her teeth on it, and it had become a sort of talisman to them both.

On the underside of a curled-over leaf, cocooned so that she could not tell if it were alive or dead, lay a caterpillar. 'The caterpillar on the leaf / Repeats to thee thy mother's grief,' she thought as she placed the leaf gently against the trellis. As she reached up the bracelet slid down to rest above her elbow and a fly, with a bravado that suggested that it knew its days were numbered anyway, alighted on the knob of her wrist bone as if it would await its quietus grazing there among the fair down. A movement of the hand sent it flying heavily on to the silvered leaf of a blighted rose. As the glassy facets of the fly's wings sparkled she felt one of those painful flashes of joy, engendered by the natural world, which have no foundation in circumstances or power to change the lives which they illumine so briefly and which give a momentary vision, too fleeting to analyse, of the universe as benign. A long arm of honeysuckle encircled her neck in a gentle green-leaved garotte. She thought she had never known an October so golden, and that if she had not emerged from so black a pit of horrors that still writhed half-forgotten in her soul she would not have been able to appreciate the gold of the day.

As she went into the house Auden's prayer that his sleeping love might find the natural world enough came into her head. That wish, that the beloved might face the light with eyes unshielded by spectacles of alcohol or dope seemed the best that one could ask. There was only one person for whom she would ask such a gift, and that was her daughter, Miranda. She had unconsciously adapted the quotation, as she discovered when she looked up the poem in the blue book whose spine had faded to dun in the dusty bookcase: it was the mortal world which the poet hoped that his love would find enough. That would do, she thought, smiling as she replaced the book, running her finger along the shelf. Today even dust did not look like an enemy.

She felt the brush of a warm coat on her bare legs as Bruno lifted his head from his bowl and trotted past her to fling himself in a pool of sun on one of the beds. Her apparel and the state of the kitchen, strewn with breakfast debris, belied the fact that Harriet had been busy since seven o'clock that morning but the black rims of her nails, as she rinsed Bruno's bowl, and piled dishes into the sink, testified to the fact that she had repotted some house plants; the loaf and margarine and smeary knives suggested she had made sandwiches for somebody; in fact for Miranda, who had caught an early train for the college where she was starting, that morning, her career as a fashion student. The sandwiches, though scorned, would, Harriet hoped, be welcome if they could be consumed in secret, out of the sight of fellow students posing as day-trippers and professors masquerading as ticket collectors and secretaries.

This was the first whole day that Harriet had had to herself for a long time and she determined not to waste it. She was going to paint, which was not only now the only activity which gave her any pleasure – and there was an enchanting tangle of flowers and leaves of berries hanging over an old wall down the road that she wanted to preserve on paper before it was desolated by winter – but was also the occupation which engendered the sluggish trickle of income which kept them afloat in the poverty to which they had become accustomed, of which Miranda did not always hide her resentment. The summer had been filled with Miranda's friends and alternately with Miranda's boredom and excitement, neither of which Harriet found conducive to working even on those rare occasions when the kitchen was empty; and she found that, as those who work at home know, the anticipation of arrivals and departures creates an enervating limbo peppered with frustration and irritability, and the failure of an awaited letter to arrive, or the telephone to ring can sour the day as hope curdles to despair.

She decided to wash the curtains before she started work and as she gathered the smoky clouds of net in her arms to place them in the machine she was reminded of Miranda's dress.

'Don't you think it's the most beautiful dress you've ever seen?' Miranda had said, pulling handfuls of grey tulle from the plastic carrier bag, a radiant conjuror about to produce her most brilliant trick. 'Isn't it the most beautiful dress in the world?'

Harriet had stared at the crumpled greenish roses mouldering on the boned bodice, with yellow stains under the arms, that rose from vapours of mothy gauze hanging over a skirt of grey tulle that time had turned to perforated zinc.

'You might be a bit more enthusiastic . . .'

'It's perfect for the party. It'll be lovely when it's had a wash.'

'I'm not going to wash it!'

Miranda beat the air from its folds and shovelled it back into the bag, and the thud of her feet on the stairs told Harriet that she had deflated and disappointed – why could she not have dredged up some spurious enthusiasm instead of flinging her own fear like a handful of grey dust over that grey dress?

The truth was, she hated the dress. It had dangled like a spectre, a mocking *memento mori* against her daughter's young face; the whisk of its skirt brought a whiff of the grave, of black lips of earth and churning worms.

It was the sort of dress that Harriet had fled from in her youth, hurtling herself down the path that had led through the years to the defeated house; and in Miranda's eyes it had the charm of an antique. Later Harriet had tried to repair the damage by praising the dress exorbitantly and asking too many questions about the party for which it had been bought.

'I probably won't go,' said Miranda.

Now it came to Harriet that she would wash the dress while Miranda was away, redeeming it as well as herself, and surprise her with its restored beauty when she came home. It was so delicate that it would have to be washed by hand, and she imagined a million trapped glittering bubbles irradiating its mesh as she lifted it white and virginal from the dirty water, the stains of another dancer's sweat of ecstasy or panic dissolving from the boned bodice, the mildewed roses unfurling plump petals as it waltzed with the October wind.

Whether it was her fault or not, Harriet was not a practical person. So much of the energy that might have been expended in kisses and fun had been frittered away in the foothills of mountains that other people took in their stride. She would have been perfectly happy painting, or lying in bed or in the garden all day smoking and reading detective stories, but love must be expressed in practical, financial and nutritional terms. She had never quite come to terms with the fact that a wall once painted, a room swept or dusted would not remain in that state. She regarded Hoovers and mops and dusters not as helpmeets but as enemies and symbols of her servitude; she was cruel to her household implements; their duties were not onerous or even very regular, but when they were called upon to perform they were often kicked and beaten. Sometimes in calm moments she had meant to observe herself to see if there was perhaps a pattern to her savagery, but she had never been sufficiently organized to correlate the evidence, and instead wept baffled tears as she clutched a bruised hand or toe and surveyed the broken plug or splintered handle that would add shame and self-inflicted pain to her resentment the next time she performed some hated chore.

As she turned to wash the breakfast dishes, in order to clear the sink for Miranda's dress, her eye caught the cream-coloured telephone clinging like a flung vanilla blancmange to the kitchen wall.

'There is not one person in the whole world who wants to speak to me,' she thought.

She was wrong. At that moment the telephone rang. It was her elderly neighbour asking, or commanding, her to go across to the shop to buy a large tin of prunes and two flat packs of soft toilet tissue. After having learned more than she wished to know about the state of the widower's intestines, and having promised to do the shopping later in the morning, she put down the phone. It rang again.

'It's only me. This is the third time I've rung. You were engaged,' the voice accused.

'Oh, hi, Mo. I'm sorry, it was my neighbour – he tends to go on a bit,' Harriet heard herself apologize.

'Never mind. What are you doing? I've got the car and I thought we could go out somewhere, it's such a lovely day. Are you still there?'

'Yes, it's just that I'm a bit tied up – there's something I want to do – some painting –'

'Oh well, if you don't want to – it was just a thought, as I've got the car . . .'

'I'd love to, really, it's just that today's the first day I've had to myself for weeks so I thought I could really get down to some work.'

'Couldn't you do it this evening? We needn't be back late.'

'Miranda will be back. It's her first day today, and I don't want to be preoccupied . . . you know how it is . . .'

'OK. It doesn't matter. I'll give you a ring later in the week. Happy painting!'

As Harriet stood with the dialling tone buzzing in the receiver in her hand, a young dustman passing the window, in a sleeveless vest, an empty bin on his shoulder, the hair under his raised arm flowering like the sooty stamens of an anemone against his white flesh, called something inaudible to her. She interpreted his greeting as condemnation of her slatternly state. Mo's disappointed voice had reduced her need to work to a selfish, self-important whim.

A small envelope, with a rustling and clatter inappropriate to its size, came through the letter box and landed on the mat. Harriet picked it up and saw a photograph of a little girl dressed in white, captioned 'The Party Dress She'll Never See', and was at once blinded herself by trite tears and muttered, 'That's all I need,' as she hid it behind a stack of letters. Reminded of Miranda's party dress she finished the dishes, and was called down from half-way up the stairs by the front-door bell. The milkman, another witness to her mid-morning disarray, lounged in the doorway watching her as she wrote the cheque. His cheekbones were embroidered with tiny amber pustules and his nails rasped on his scalp as he pushed back his cap to scratch in his hair; she winced at the thought of those nails on the silver-foil milk bottle tops.

When he had gone she determined not to let the impulse to work dissipate and wiped the kitchen table, which was the only surface big enough, and set out paper, paints and brushes and a jam jar of water and tried to dissolve her guilt at Mo's disappointed voice in the clear water that held the faintest turquoise tinge reflected from the walls of glass that confined it and spawned spiralling strings of minuscule bubbles like glass beads. 'I'll put Miranda's dress to soak,' she thought, 'have a quick bath and get dressed, go to the shop and have another look at the plants on that wall and then start work. I don't believe it!'

The phone was ringing again.

The voice that came through was furred-up, like an old waste-pipe, with whisky.

'Dad.'

'I thought you might have rung yesterday to see how I got on at the hospital.'

Oh God. She had forgotten all about it.

'I did ring. All the lines to Rottingdean were busy. How did you get on?'

Her heart was banging about in the old painful way. She drummed her fingers on the marrow which lay on the table radiating vegetable calm from its green and yellow stripes.

'I didn't go!'

His triumphant crow was splattered against her ear in an eruption of wet coughing. She held the receiver at arm's length.

'Why didn't you? Did they change your appointment?'

'I was dressed and waiting for that sodding ambulance at eight o'clock. Do you know what time they turned up? Gone eleven. I told them what they could do with their bloody appointment.'

'I bet that showed the bastards,' said Harriet wearily, realizing that she would have to apologize, make a new appointment and accompany him.

'What? Showed the bastards, didn't I? Who do they think they are?'

'I expect some of them think they're people who are trying to do a very unpleasant job with very little money, or resources.'

It didn't matter what she said, he would neither hear nor remember.

'Bloody hospitals.'

'You chose not to know when I was in hospital.'

'How would you know, you've never been in hospital. Except when Miranda was born, I suppose. Anyway, I just thought you'd be interested to hear how I got on.'

'Fascinated.'

'Has she gone back to school? You said she was coming to see me in the holidays. When's she coming?'

'I'm not sure. Soon . . .'

'What?'

'I don't know, Dad. She's a big girl now, I can't force –'

'What do you mean, force?' – he had heard that all right. 'You're just jealous of Miranda and me. Just because I'm old and ill. You'll find out one day, when you're old and ill and nobody wants to know . . .'

'It's not *just* because you're old and ill, Dad, it's because you're also boring and disgusting and totally selfish.'

Her words were lost in his coughing.

'Listen, Dad. I'll come to see you tomorrow. Can you hear me, Dad? SEE YOU TOMORROW. I'LL BRING SOME LUNCH.'

'Nobody bloody cares if I go to the hospital or not. The nurses don't care, the doctors don't care, you don't care . . .'

'If you ever looked at me, if you had the slightest interest in, or conception of what my life has been like, you would see that I had nothing left to care *with*. Why should I care? For a moment's carelessness on your part and a few miserable years I have to pay in blood for the rest of my life.'

'Harriet, are you still there? Harry?'

'I said, I'll SEE YOU TOMORROW. GOODBYE, DAD, I'VE GOT TO GO, THERE'S SOMEONE AT THE DOOR.'

She went to answer it with an image in her mind of herself and her father, writhing in their separate torment, joined across the miles by an inseverable twisted plastic cord.

'Ms James?'

A young woman in jeans and a short overall bearing the logo of a local flower shop was holding out a huge cellophane cone of flowers rosetted with yellow ribbon.

'No. I mean, I'll take them for her,' Harriet lied, realizing that it would be inconceivable to the girl that anyone should send flowers to a person such as herself. But he had, and she knew who he was without reading the card.

'The last bloody straw.'

She propped up the sheaf of flowers in the kitchen, lit a cigarette – the first one of the day, as she congratulated herself – and ran upstairs to Miranda's room. The dress hung from a wire hanger, and Harriet was caught by a rush of love for the body that would fill it, the bony shoulders that would rise from the stained bodice, the downy arms. 'Let her be happy,' she prayed, and was assaulted by the memory of a very small girl saying with such vehemence, 'Mummy, when you go to Heaven, I'm going to *cling* on to you and fly up with you,' that she could still feel those fingers digging into her flesh.

She gathered the dress to her, as she would have liked to embrace her daughter, and the tip of her cigarette caught a fold and a tongue of flame leaped up the gauze, and died, leaving a hideous black valley up the centre of the skirt.

Her carelessness. Her carelessness that amounted to cruelty – her stupidity that might be misinterpreted as spite – she pulled the folds together as if the damage would disappear and opened them to display the blackened horror. The burn might come out when she washed it and perhaps she could mend – there was no white, or grey thread – get some when she went for the prunes and toilet paper. If only she hadn't interfered, had let well alone – Miranda hadn't wanted it washed – if she hadn't lit that stupid cigarette – it was all to prove her love – all for herself. She stood in the smell of scorched dust cradling the corpse of her attempt at redemption.

In the kitchen, the net curtains, which had not been burned, tumbled careless gouts of foam through the black outlet hose into the sink. Harriet laid the dress in the washing-up bowl and turned on the taps gently and scattered detergent like someone dropping earth on a coffin. As she watched, the stems of the roses unwound in slimy slow motion and the petals disengaged one by one as the glue dissolved, and floated separately on the surface of the water.

The door bell rang.

'Go away,' she screamed.

It rang again.

'Who is it?'

'Gas meter.'

'Can't you come back later?'

'No.'

'In a few minutes –' she pleaded, tearing at her hair with sudsy hands.

'I've got to –' The rest of his words were lost as she wrenched the door open. He stepped into the kitchen and smiled round at the disorder, the sun striking brassy notes in his cadmium-yellow hair.

'Caught you on the hop, did I?'

Harriet stared at him, thinking that the black tufts in his nose, contrasting so blatantly with his hair, effectively cancelled out the charm that he so obviously thought he possessed, and caused the cheeky grin to lose its confidence. How could anyone be so mistaken about himself? At least she was aware of every aspect of her unkempt looks and dowdy *déshabillé*.

'Who's a lucky girl then?' He indicated the flowers. 'Someone's birthday today?' She glared at him as if distaste would turn the bunches of hair into iron filings and choke him. She saw the stems of the flowers protruding from his mouth, his throat jammed with cellophane. She slammed on the radio.

'Mind if I use your toilet?'

She pointed silently upwards, then pushed past him and ran upstairs but had time only to claw a heap of Miranda's night things from the floor, drape a wet towel over the rail and glimpse a nailbrush and sponge stranded in the bubbles dying in the bath and retrieve a pair of espadrilles from the basin before he was standing at the lavatory, waiting for her to leave. Bruno padded in and sniffed at his ankles; Harriet shooed him away.

Downstairs, shreds of gauze came away in her hands, and as she acknowledged that the dress was disintegrating, the young man returned. He squatted down in front of the cupboard, shining his torch into the cluttered interior, then started scrabbling objects out on to the floor.

'Bit of a glory hole, innit?' he remarked, cheerfully piling up cobwebbed cake tins, a broken cup and saucer, the split plastic bag of Christmas cake decorations which scattered around him. Then, whistling along with the radio, he raked out empty bottles and stood them in a semicircle round his haunches. Harriet could have explained that they were the accumulation of past months of drinking, waiting to be taken to the bottle bank in a friend's car, that she had not in fact had a drink for weeks, but the bottles stood in a silent green hostile crowd and any defence that she offered would be contradicted by these glass perjurers. One, she saw, bore a label that said Goldener Oktober, like the golden October day that had been wrecked.

'All I wanted to do today was paint a bloody little picture,' she thought. She looked at the twin shiny patches on the seat of his grey trousers. 'How dare he force his way in here and rake through my life?'

All her self-hatred was directed at the slight figure in the inglorious uniform. She grabbed the marrow, lifted it high with both hands, and he received the full weight of the ruined dress, the empty bottles and the years of failure and despair on the back of his head.

She stepped back as he sprawled slowly sideways and the bottles fell like skittles around him. One rolled to her feet, almost full, splashing purple on to the floor as a bright red sticky gout dyed his yellow hair. His hand closed on a plastic reindeer. Harriet picked up the bottle and as she gulped the purple vinegar sprayed her face and dressing gown and the shiny grey jacket. She forced the wine down her throat against the rising nausea. She knew she must obscure with a purple haze the enormity of what she had done; the widow and orphans and bereaved parents and siblings she had created with one mad blow. The room became darker as if the alcohol had created its own twilight. Her resistance was low and her ears were filling with purple cotton wool. A fly, like the one which had grazed on her wrist in the garden, settled on the fallen man's head as if on a luscious yellow flower oozing red nectar, and that final violation of the innocent violater was more than she could bear. She rushed from room to room getting ready to leave for ever, finally grabbing her purse and tying the first thing that came to hand to Bruno's collar, finished the wine and leaving the radio buzzing away on low batteries, the washing machine throbbing in its final spin, the sheathed flowers a cone of blurred colour lying across a heap of bottles, the man sprawled on the floor among the Christmas cake decorations and Miranda's dress in the washing-up bowl, slammed the front door behind her.

On her way to the station she lurched unbelievingly against the old brick wall that she had meant to paint, long ago, that morning, in an irrecoverable guiltlessness. Only yesterday it had been hung with hearts, a tangle of convolvulus, nightshade, elderberries, snowberries and ivy. Now all the white bells and berries and green hearts were gone and she traced with her finger the fuzzy scars that laced the wall where the ivy had been ripped from the brick. At the end of the wall, through the rolled-up door, she saw a man with silver hair standing on a stepladder, whistling as he painted the interior of his garage. A rage possessed her at the sight of the neatly stacked tools and tins on his shelves, that someone's life should be so well ordered that he had to fill his time by painting the inside of a garage. The garden wall which had been so beautiful had been desecrated as she, who had once been beautiful, was ruined. She walked into the garage and kicked away the steps, hearing a scream as he fell to the concrete floor.

Bruno was dragging at his lead and she had to pick him up and carry him. As they crossed the road they passed one of Miranda's friends, a girl with long fair hair falling about her shoulders. Harriet was transfixed by the knowledge that the girl must grow old and die. ' "All her bright golden hair/

Tarnished with rust,/She that was young and fair/Fallen to dust," ' she told her as a milk float screeched at her, frightening Bruno and fluttering her skirt. She couldn't remember where she was supposed to be going, only that it must be somewhere very peaceful, a haven out of the swing of the sea. 'I have asked to be where no storms come . . .' She couldn't remember. 'Not Rottingdean,' she said, 'definitely not Rottingdean.'

She swayed into the station. There were two station staff who looked so alike that they might have been brothers: one was friendly and cheerful and the other sullen. Harriet encountered one of them in the booking hall.

'Are you the nice one, or the other one?'

He did not reply.

'I want a ticket to Innisfree, to the Lake Isle. I shall find some peace there.'

She wandered down the platform and sat down on a bench. She was aware that her bracelet was missing and was conscious at the time of a blacker grief but it was like trying to fit together the pieces of a grotesque jigsaw whose edges are slippery with blood, and then the darkness became absolute as she closed her eyes.

When a dream becomes unbearable the sleeper awakes. Harriet struggled through blackness, with the alarm clock shrilling like a siren in her ears, to the blessed realization that the monstrous epic which she had lived through had been only a nightmare.

'Thank God,' she said as she pushed Bruno from her chest and sat up in the disoriented dawn, shaking her head to dislodge three uniformed figures on the edge of her headache, blinking away the last remnant of the dream.

They made straight for her. After all it was not difficult to spot, on a station platform, a woman in a pink towelling dressing gown splashed with wine, clutching a cat on the end of a string of bloody tinsel.

'It was an accident,' she mumbled as the policewoman pulled her to her feet.

'One man is dead and another in hospital, and you're saying it was an accident?'

Harriet blinked at them in bleary bewilderment.

'The dress – it was an accident.'

Slaves to the Mushroom

'OVERALLS, ladies!'

That was the signal for the work-force to peel off its rubber gloves, remove its protective clothing and down tools and hurry across to the new canteen, where the wearing of overalls was forbidden.

'And gentleman,' added the supervisor, catching the offended eye of Robbo, the only male worker who wore one of the firm's issue green and white gingham nylon smocks, his crinkly hair tied back in a matching checked bandeau.

The morning break lasted ten minutes and workers were faced with a choice of visiting the cloakroom or the canteen; the buildings were several hundred yards apart and although there might just be time to queue for a cup of tea, after a visit to the toilet there would not be time to drink it. Robbo and his friend Billy headed for the cloakroom, jumping over the trough of disinfectant that everybody was supposed to walk through on leaving the shed.

Some people had been working all night and were due to knock off for the day. Others had started their shifts at seven or eight o'clock, and the canteen served a good breakfast menu; toast, eggs, bacon, sausages, tinned tomatoes, fruit juice, tea and coffee. The workers sat at yellow formica-topped tables and flicked their cigarette ash into silver-foil ashtrays. Although the food was cheap, some workers, those Asian women for example who did not prefer to huddle in the cloakroom, brought their own food and thermos flasks.

Sylvia carried her tray over to the nearest table where a group of people who had just started that week sat together and, finding herself opposite a black man with an artificial hand, saw an opportunity to tell the story of how, when hunting as a girl, a hound had bitten off her nipple. He was unimpressed, stirring his tea arrogantly with the spoon held in a sort of pincer.

'They're called dogs,' he said.

'Well, this was definitely a hound,' replied Sylvia huffily. 'I should know.'

The canteen was clean and warm; outside the aluminium-framed windows sleet was whipped about a dirty-looking sky. Spanish words and laughter from a table of black-haired women chalked up the most decibels and was rivalled by Urdu or some such from the large sari-ed contingent, who were bussed in by their own coach. Sylvia decided to forgive the man, and give him and his fellow newcomers a friendly word of warning. She lowered her voice.

'You have to watch those Asians,' she said. 'They take your mushrooms if you don't keep an eye on them. Lean right across the beds and grab all the best ones. Work in gangs, they do, go up and down cutting the big ones. No wonder they always get such big bonuses. We don't stand a chance. You've got to watch them.'

'How long have you been working here?' a girl asked.

'Fortnight pay day.'

The supervisors whistled up their teams and tea break was over. A drift of icing sugar lay over the leaves and a flash of February sun gilded the icy puddles in the gravel as they crunched back in their wellies to the sheds, throwing half-smoked cigarettes into the bin of sand outside the door.

*

Green Star Mushrooms Limited was a member of a large group of companies and supplied chains of pizza restaurants, stores and supermarkets as well as having numerous smaller outlets for its white cultured fungi. It consisted of an administration block, a building that housed generators and machinery, storage and packaging depots and six vast windowless sheds like aircraft hangars where the mushrooms grew. Each shed was divided into four sections, and each section housed four long bays, each in four tiers, like aluminium bunk beds packed with compost. To pick from the lowest bed, workers had to crouch on the floor; aluminium stepladders were used to reach the second and third levels, and the top bed was attained by a central flight of steps, and when all the pickers were installed up there, a section of the walkway was slid over the entrance and nobody could come down again until it was removed. A long polythene wind-tunnel was suspended just above their heads. Swinging about like monkeys was frowned on. The sheds seemed dark until you became accustomed to the electric light.

'Right. Everybody into number thirteen,' Shirley the supervisor called.

'Lucky for some,' said Robbo.

Sylvia stuck her number on the boxes and baskets she had picked and unhooked her ladder and tray and bucket and made for the door. She was dismayed to see the heaps and piles of boxes and baskets the Asians were staggering along with. That pretty little girl who had started on the same day as she smiled at her as she put down her pyramid. They had been friends for a morning until she had been enveloped in the silken cluster of her own kind, and now unless she smiled Sylvia could not recognize her. They all looked alike, with their long black plaits down their backs, except those whose plaits were grey.

'Hello, Sheila,' said Sylvia, thinking again that it was a sensible English-sounding name.

'Hi, Sylvia,' said Shreela. 'How many pounds have you picked this morning?'

'Enough,' said Sylvia, standing on tiptoe to hoist her heavy bucket of stalks and broken mushrooms and compost and empty it into the huge polythene sack on a frame provided for waste. She could see who was going to get a bonus and who wasn't. Shirley and an assistant stood at the door weighing them and noting down each person's pickings.

No mushrooms were allowed to be taken from one room to another; neither was any equipment without first being sterilized. Stepladders had to be dunked into a vat of disinfectant, first one way up, and then the other, likewise trays and knives. The floor was awash with suds and stalks and bits of mushroom; there were men whose job it was to keep the floors clean, and to empty the rubbish sacks. Sylvia wondered what became of the stalks, wondered if they were utilized in some way. It seemed such a waste; surely they could be used to make packet soup or something; great vats of grey soup ladled out to the homeless and hungry. She had decided not to ask, since her enquiry as to what the compost consisted of was met with the short answer 'shit'. It was better not to think about that; the crumbly dark compost smelled of mildew and nothing worse, but she imagined it was shovelled out from battery houses where chickens were kept in cruel and grotesque captivity; she had seen one once on a visit to a farm and the smell had been overpoweringly disgusting. The battery was not unlike this place, she thought.

'At least we've got room to turn around and flap our wings,' she remarked to the women waiting to dunk their ladders.

'Pardon?'

'Sylvia, you're dreaming again. Get on with it.' Shirley had materialized in her white official wellies. Sylvia's knife slipped from her fingers and fell to the bottom of the vat. She had to roll up her sleeve and plunge her arm in, but she couldn't reach the bottom. She panicked, flapping her wet arms about. This was total disaster. She didn't know whether to run away, out of the shed into the bleak countryside never to return, or to try to manage without her knife, but there was no way she could break the stalks off as neatly as she could cut them. She was elbowed out of the way and was making desperate bids to reach the knife, leaning right over the murky water until she almost fell in, her face scraping the surface. Someone grasped her ankles. Sylvia screamed, flailing about, certain that she was to be drowned. Then she felt the ground beneath her feet and turned to scream at her attacker. It was Dexter towering over her, grinning.

'Looking for something?'

She would have given him a piece of her mind but she saw Shirley approaching.

'My knife,' she gasped. 'I dropped it.'

Dexter reached down and effortlessly brought out the knife, his brown arm dripping dirty pearls. Sylvia could have kissed it. She scuttled off to number thirteen, her ladder with her rack hooked over it and a pile of boxes and baskets clanking behind her. She had been late clocking on, having to change into her wellies, and the only ladder left had been this rusty job with one wheel. Funny how she always got lumbered with the leftovers. As now, when she arrived in the shed, everybody else had nabbed the best places. She was confronted with a sparse sprinkling of tiny mushrooms in the only vacant bed.

'What are we picking?' she asked the woman next to her, who with her friend formed a deadly team. They had been there only as long as Sylvia but had already chalked up fat bonuses and were due to be promoted to Valerie's team of skilled pickers. Sylvia would have to wait the statutory six weeks before promotion and the rate she was going, might not achieve it even then.

'Down to 5p,' said the woman. Sylvia received the news glumly. It took her for ever to fill a box with these hateful buttons. The closed mushrooms were categorized according to size – 5p, 10p and 50p, large and extra large. 'If we got five pence for each mushroom we picked, that would work out at more than £2.30 an hour, wouldn't it?'

Nobody answered.

'Fives into £2.30 goes – forty-six. So that's forty-six

mushrooms per hour, I mean pence per mushroom we ought to get, isn't it, Marie?'

Again Marie didn't bother to answer Batty Sylvia, who went on happily with her calculations while her basket remained empty.

'Fifty pence per mushroom, now that would be, um, £2.30 divided by fifty equals, knock off the noughts and that's 4⅗ per mushroom, we ought to get . . .'

'Something a bit wrong with your calculations, gel.'

It was that Dexter strutting along in his tight jeans like a cockerel in a yard of hens.

'Don't you gel me,' said Sylvia crossly, then she remembered he had retrieved her knife.

'Dexter! Sylvia! Get on with your work.'

Someone made a ribald noise.

Sylvia blushed. Having her name shouted out like that as if she was a naughty little girl in school, by a chit of a girl half her age. She bowed her head over the bed and started cutting mushrooms, but her heart was thudding as she saw Shirley approach.

'I dread it when I see those white wellies coming,' muttered Robbo who was working the opposite side of her bed, where she could see great clusters of fifty-pence mushrooms disappearing under his knife. Sylvia liked best the open mushrooms, big as saucers, big as elephant's ears: half a dozen of them filled a basket; they were more like the mushrooms she had found in the fields as a girl in the early morning or the evening with the rough grass silvered and wet with dew.

'What are these?' Shirley was shaking the box.

'My buttons,' said Sylvia.

'Why are they in a box? You know buttons go in a basket. Where are your ten pences?'

'Here,' Sylvia held out a green plastic box. A few mushrooms rolled about on the bottom.

'You've got your open and your closed mixed up. And they're supposed to be of uniform size. Get them sorted out, and get your act together.'

Act? Sylvia's back felt as if it was breaking, her knees creaked as she crouched. She lapsed on to her knees, feeling wet mud seep through her trousers. She picked until she had exhausted that bed and then unhooked her rack from the side of the bed, folded up her ladder and carried them, with her boxes and baskets to another bed. She had forgotten her numbers, a roll of sticky labels that had to be stuck on every box and basket that she picked, so that her quota could be assessed. She found them lying in a muddy pool. Everything was so mucky, the fingers of her rubber gloves were engrained with sticky black mould, her sleeve stinking of disinfectant, her wellies bleared, her overall had a wet dirty patch right across the stomach and there was a smear of compost on her cheek. Some people managed to look quite neat and composed at the end of the day; not Sylvia. She was wrecked by dinner time. If you didn't wear your rubber gloves your fingers were stained and your nails packed with black mould that a scrubbing brush could not remove. Like the supermarket trolley which inevitably Sylvia got, the one with the squeak and the wheels that went in the wrong direction, her ladder was unstable and her rack hung at a perilous angle, endangering her mushrooms. Pull, slice off the stalk, mushroom in box or basket, stalk in bucket, stoop, bend, up the ladder, stretch, pull, cut, down the ladder, empty bucket. Nobody was talking much today, except the Asian women who talked incessantly. It was amazing that anybody could have so much to say. To Sylvia's eye they moved like a flock of brightly coloured locusts leaving the beds bare behind them.

'It's not fair,' she complained to Shirley. 'They're picking all the mushrooms.'

'That's what they're paid to do.'

Talk about inverted prejudice.

Later, however, she was pleased to hear Shirley telling them off for indiscriminate picking, dropping everything into their baskets regardless of size, and appointing two of their number to sort them out. Downright cheating.

Getting her act together: Sylvia saw all the mushroom

pickers in a Busby Berkeley-style sequence, turning their buckets upside down and beating them like drums, swarming up the aluminium supports like sailors in the rigging, kicking out their arms and legs starwise, their green and white gingham overalls twirling as they tap-danced in their wellies, juggling mushrooms and flashing knives, spreading out the pink palms of their rubber glovers as they fell on one knee behind Shirley, the star in her white wellies.

'Where's your radio, Sharon?' she called.

'Pardon?'

'I said, where's your wireless today?'

'I left it in the toilet.'

'Go and get it then.'

'I can't.'

'Go on.'

'You go and get it if you're so keen.'

Sylvia knew there was no way she could leave the shed. On her first morning she had heard someone who asked to go to the toilet told that she should have gone at tea break.

' "Radio Mercury, the heart of the South," ' she sang in compensation, and then,

> 'You and me, we sweat and strain
> Bodies all achin', wracked with pain
> Tote dat barge, lift dat bale –
> Get a little drunk and you lands in jai-aal.'

Robbo joined in in a surprising bass voice, given the overall and bandeau, and then he and Billy dissolved into cackles. It wasn't that funny, thought Sylvia, but she was glad she had made them laugh. Sometimes this place was like a morgue with everyone silently picking, lost in their own thoughts and in the smell of mildew. Then Shirley came along and detailed Sylvia and a silent lad named Gary to clear one of the beds that had been picked. People were supposed to clear the beds as they went along, but this one was full of a debris of broken stalks and deformed mushrooms and frail thin toadstools, illegal immigrants who had sneaked in somehow. Gary didn't mind, he mooned through the day, pale as a mushroom, just achieving his quota and never thinking of a bonus, but Sylvia was seething on the top step of her rickety ladder as she grubbed out the leftovers, losing valuable picking time while others filled their baskets with mushrooms that should have been hers.

'What's for dinner, Stewart?' called Marie.

Stewart couldn't read or write but he always knew the menu off by heart.

'Sausage, beans and chips. Quiche and salad. Macaroni cheese. Fruit slice and custard or ice cream.' He spoke thickly as though his mouth was already crammed with bangers and beans.

Sylvia looked at her watch. It had drowned in the disinfectant and presented a bloated, dead face.

'Right, bring your mushrooms to be checked and go to dinner.'

The newcomers who had not yet been issued with gloves had to scrub their hands in the trough in the passage. Sylvia hurried past them, through the footbath and into the fresh freezing air, narrowly missing a forklift truck, and lighting a cigarette as she went and joined the queue in the canteen. Maintenance men and the other workers were already seated at some of the tables. She carried her tray over to an empty table where she was joined by Marie and her mate, Dexter, Stewart and Sharon.

'Ooooh, my back. It's killing me. When I took this job I'd no idea there'd be so much heavy lifting.'

'And carrying. And climbing.'

'What did you do before?' Marie asked Sylvia.

'Oh, all sorts of things. Shop work, bar work, kennel maid . . .'

'I'm surprised you wanted to work with dogs, after what that hound did to you.'

'Oh well, it didn't mean any harm. Just got overexcited.'

A guffaw of crude laughter greeted this. Sylvia concentrated on threading a piece of macaroni on each of the tines of her fork. She hated vulgarity, and besides the incident had not happened to her but to somebody else she had heard of.

'I was working in a Christmas-cracker factory up until a few weeks ago.'

'Why d'you give it up?'

'Oh, the novelty wore off.'

She might have added that she had a job in a balloon factory, but she blew it, and that she used to work in a pub until she was barred, she had been a postwoman but she got the sack, and that she had worked on a newspaper but it folded. That hadn't been her fault; she was just the tea lady. She had to work, Jack couldn't and she had to support them both. She didn't like leaving him alone all day, but it couldn't be helped.

'I picked fifty-eight pounds this morning,' she heard someone say. 'What did you do?'

'Fifty-three.'

You could buy mushrooms cheap if you wanted, on Friday afternoons, but to do that would have meant Sylvia's missing the firm's minibus which dropped her at the top of her road. Anyway she hadn't felt like eating a mushroom since she started this job; even a mug of mushroom soup brought on a bout of nausea. She had had a narrow escape on her first morning. Shirley had come up to her and said, 'You're not eating mushrooms are you?'

'No, I'm chewing gum.'

'Well, you're not really supposed to eat in here at all.'

'Sorry.'

Phew. A few minutes before, she had been eating mushrooms, popping the little white buttons into her mouth as she worked, just as one eats strawberries when strawberry picking. Now the nasty monopods clodhopped through her dreams, and the smell of the compost was enough to turn her up. One old bloke, with one eye, did eat the mushrooms, but he was the only one, and she was sure Shirley turned a blind eye.

Just before the half-hour was up, Sylvia made a dash for the cloakroom. She didn't bother with make-up any more, or to comb her hair. Every pair of trousers she possessed was stained at the knees with brown marks that wouldn't wash out, and she was too tired to care. After her first day her arms had been so stiff that she could hardly move them, her back felt as if it was broken and her legs felt as heavy as trees. She was getting used to it now, and managing quite well with just the fractured spine. As she emerged from the ladies' cloakroom she encountered Robbo and Billy coming giggling out of the gents'.

What have you two been up to?' she asked in a friendly fashion, but they didn't answer. Nevertheless she was pleased to follow them because she had forgotten which shed they were in, and they all looked alike to her. There had been the awful time she had left her numbers in the canteen and had to gallop back to get them, only to find they had been put in the dinner waste, and she had had to rake through a refuse sack of banana skins and cigarette butts and slimy yoghurt cartons and half-eaten sandwiches to find them, and then she had run back to the wrong shed and wandered for what seemed hours like a lost soul through all the wrong sheds opening doors on silent beds of ghostly mushrooms, and throbbing machinery and men hosing down the floors. She was crying when she finally found her team. She was supposed to be working on the top stage and the trap door had been shut, and people had had to move all their ladders and baskets and boxes to let her in, and of course all those people who worked in gangs and pairs had grabbed all the best places.

Half-way through the afternoon they had to change sheds again, so racks were unhooked, ladders folded and perilous pyramids of boxes and baskets carried to be weighed. Sylvia had done a bit better since lunch and was feeling quite pleased with herself as she dunked her stepladder in the disinfectant, first this way, then that. Sharon had brought her radio and the afternoon was passing quite pleasantly until Billy started teasing Stewart about living in a hostel.

'What sort of a hostel is it then?' he kept saying.

'It's for the handicapped,' Stewart said.

'Why d'you live there then, Stewart?'

'Leave him alone,' someone shouted.

'Pick on someone your own size,' suggested somebody else and everybody laughed. Billy was a slender five feet two, and Stewart was a lumbering six feet, bursting out of his cardigan. Then Billy started jostling Stewart and knocked a basket of his mushrooms to the floor. Stewart gave a howl as they rolled away in the mess of muddy compost and stalks and lunged at Billy with his knife. The man with the artificial arm leaped forward and seized the knife in a lightning pincer grasp. Stewart fell to his knees snuffling as he gathered up his dirty mushrooms, like precious jewels, and replaced them in his basket.

'It'd serve you right if I had an epileptic fit,' he told Billy.

'Robbo. Billy. Outside.' Shirley's white wellies had sped silently down the aisle. Robbo and Billy followed them out to the tune of 'Rat in the Kitchen' from Sharon's radio.

'They're for the chop,' said Dexter. 'Tippling on the job again.'

In the administrative block Robbo and Billy faced the boss in her white cap with the Green Star insignia. Robbo had removed his bandeau and his hair spread out on the shoulders of his green and white overall.

'By the way,' he said, 'remember when I cut myself with my knife?'

'You'd had your tetanus jabs,' interrupted Shirley.

'It bled quite a lot if you remember, all over the place . . . all over my mushrooms.'

'Well?'

'Well, I just wondered if I should have mentioned that I was AIDS positive . . .?'

He and Billy departed laughing to pick up their cards,

leaving the two women to ponder the credibility and implications of his statement.

'Five o'clock people, pack up your things.'

As she carried her things to the door Sylvia saw little Sheila's silky trousers coming down the steps from the top bed. That was all she could see of her, so hung about with brimming baskets and piled with full green boxes was she. It was unbelievable. Sylvia had worked really hard, and Sheila's efforts made it look as though she hadn't tried at all.

'You've done well, Sheila,' said Sylvia. 'Let me give you a hand with some of those.'

She put down her own poor pickings and took some of Shreela's from her.

'Oh, thank you, Sylvia. If you just take these for me I'll go and get the rest.' The rest. Sylvia knelt quickly and peeled off Shreela's numbers from four of the boxes and stuck on her own. Then she piled them on top of her boxes and carried them to be weighed. She could see that Shirley was impressed as she wrote down the amount. Then she went back to help Shreela with the rest of her load. She joined the queue to wash the stepladder, wash the rack, stack them up, then dashed to the cloakroom for her coat. No time to change out of her wellies. The minibus was waiting. If Fred was driving, you were allowed to smoke; if the other Fred was driving, you weren't.

As the Green Star minibus snouted out into the lane Sylvia reflected that she would have lots to tell Jack when she got home – Billy and Robbo getting the chop, Dexter rescuing her knife, her bumper crop; and he would tell her all about his day, the tussle with a spray of millet, hard pecking on the cuttlefish, conversations with himself in the mirror. She wondered what to have for tea; whatever it was, it wouldn't be mushrooms on toast. Behind them in the sheds, thousands of tiny white nodules no bigger than a pin's head starring the black compost were starting to swell.

Cardboard City

'WE could always pick the dog hairs off each other's coats . . .'

The thought of grooming each other like monkeys looking for fleas sent them into giggles – anything would have.

'I used half a roll of Sellotape on mine,' said Stella indignantly then, although she wasn't really offended.

'It better not have been my Sellotape or I'll kill you,' Vanessa responded, without threat.

'It was His.'

'Good. *He'll* kill you then,' she said matter-of-factly.

The sisters, having flung themselves on to the train with no time to buy a comic, were wondering how to pass the long minutes until it reached central London with nothing to read. They could hardly believe that at the last moment He had not contrived to spoil their plan to go Christmas shopping. For the moment it didn't matter that their coats were unfashionable and the cuffs of their acrylic sweaters protruded lumpishly from the outgrown sleeves or that their frozen feet were beginning to smart, in the anticipation of chilblains, in their scuffed shoes in reaction to the heater under the seat. They were alone in the compartment except for a youth with a personal stereo leaking a tinny rhythm through the headphones.

With their heavy greenish-blonde hair cut straight across their foreheads and lying flat as lasagne over the hoods and shoulders of their school duffles, and their green eyes set wide apart in the flat planes of their pale faces, despite Stella's borrowed fishnet stockings which were causing her much *Angst*, they looked younger than their fourteen and twelve years. It would not have occurred to either of them that anybody staring at them might have been struck by anything other than their horrible clothes. Their desire, thwarted by Him and by lack of money of their own, was to look like everybody else. The dog hairs that adhered so stubbornly to the navy-blue cloth and bristled starkly in the harsh and electric light of the winter morning were from Barney, the black and white border collie, grown fat and snappish in his old age, who bared his teeth at his new master, the usurper, and slunk into a corner at his homecoming, as the girls slunk into their bedroom.

'It's cruel to keep that animal alive,' He would say. 'What's it got to live for? Smelly old hearthrug.'

And while He discoursed on the Quality of Life, running a finger down Mummy's spine or throat, Barney's legs would splay out worse than they usually did and his claws click louder on the floor, or a malodorous cloud of stagnant pond water emanate from his coat. It was a sign of His power that Barney was thus diminished.

'We'll know when the Time has come. And the Time has not yet come,' said Mummy with more energy than she summoned to champion her elder daughters, while Barney rolled a filmy blue eye in her direction. The dog, despite his shedding coat, was beyond reproach as far as the girls were concerned; his rough back and neck had been salted with many tears, and he was their one link with their old life, before their father had disappeared and before their mother had defected to the enemy.

'What are you going to buy Him?' Vanessa asked.

'Nothing. I'm making His present.'

'What?' Vanessa was incredulous, fearing treachery afoot.

'I'm knitting Him a pair of socks. Out of stinging nettles.'

'I wish I could knit.'

After a wistful pause she started to say, 'I wonder what He would . . .'

'I'm placing a total embargo on His name today,' Stella cut her off. 'Don't speak of Him. Don't even think about Him. Right, Regan?'

'Right, Goneril. Why does He call us those names?'

'They're the Ugly Sisters in Cinderella of course.'

'I thought they were called Anastasia and . . . and . . .'

'Embargo,' said Stella firmly.

'It's not Cordelia who needs a fairy godmother, it's us. Wouldn't it be lovely if one day . . .'

'Grow up.'

So that was how He saw them, bewigged and garishly rouged, two pantomine dames with grotesque beauty spots and fishnet tights stretched over their bandy men's calves, capering jealously round Cordelia's high chair. Cordelia herself, like Barney, was adored unreservedly, but after her birth, with one hand rocking the transparent hospital cot in which she lay, as a joke which they could not share, He had addressed her half-sisters as Goneril and Regan. Their mother had protested then, but now sometimes she used the names. Under His rule, comfortable familiar objects vanished and routines were abolished. Exposed to His mockery, they became ludicrous. One example was the Bunnykins china they ate from sometimes, not in a wish to prolong their babyhood but because it was there. All the pretty mismatched bits and pieces of crockery were superseded by a stark white service from Habitat and there were new forks with vicious prongs and knives which cut. Besotted with Cordelia's dimples and black curls, He lost all patience with his step-daughters, with their tendency to melancholy and easily provoked tears which their pink eyelids and noses could not conceal, and like a vivisector with an electric prod tormenting two albino mice, he discovered all their most vulnerable places.

Gypsies had travelled up in the train earlier, making their buttonholes and nosegays, and had left the seats and floor strewn with a litter of twigs and petals and scraps of silver foil like confetti.

'We might see Princess Di or Fergie,' Vanessa said, scuffing the debris with her foot. 'They do their Christmas shopping in Harrods.'

'The Duchess of York to you. Oh yes, we're sure to run into them. Anyway, Princess Diana does her shopping in Covent Garden.'

'Well then!' concluded Vanessa triumphantly. She noticed the intimation of a cold sore on her sister's superior lip and was for a second glad. Harrods and Covent Garden were where they had decided, last night, after lengthy discussions, to go, their excited voices rising from guarded whispers to a normal pitch, until He had roared upstairs at them to shut up. Vanessa's desire to go to Hamleys had been overruled. She had cherished a secret craving for a tube of plastic stuff with which you blew bubbles and whose petroleum smell she found as addictive as the smell of new Elastoplast. Now she took out her purse and checked her ticket and counted her money yet again. Even with the change she had filched fearfully from the trousers He had left sprawled across the bedroom chair, it didn't amount to much. Stella was rich, as the result of her paper round and the tips she had received in return for the cards she had put through her customers' doors wishing them a 'Merry Christmas from your Newsboy/Newsgirl,' with a space for her to sign her name. She would have been even wealthier had He not demanded the money for the repair of the iron whose flex had burst into flames in her hand while she was ironing His shirt. She could not see how it had been her fault but supposed it must have been. The compartment filled up at each stop and the girls stared out of the window rather than speak in public, or look at each other and see mirrored in her sister her own unsatisfactory self.

The concourse at Victoria was scented with sweet and sickening melted chocolate from a booth that sold fresh-baked cookies, and crowded with people criss-crossing each other with loaded trolleys, running to hurl themselves at the barriers, dragging luggage and children; queuing helplessly for tickets while the minutes to departure ticked away, swirling round the bright scarves outside the Tie Rack, panic-buying festive socks and glittery bow ties, slurping coffee and beer and champing croissants and pizzas and jacket potatoes and trying on earrings. It had changed so much from the last time they had seen it that only the late arrival of their train and the notice of cancellation and delay on the indicator board reassured them that they were at the right Victoria Station.

'I've got to go to the Ladies.'

'OK.'

Vanessa attempted to join the dismayingly long queue trailing down the stairs but Stella had other plans.

'Stell-a! Where are you going?' She dragged Vanessa into the side entrance of the Grosvenor Hotel.

'Stella, we can't! It's a HOTEL! We'll be ARRESTED . . .' She wailed as Stella's fingers pinched through her coat sleeves, propelling her up the steps and through the glass doors.

'Shut up. Look as though we're meeting somebody.'

Vanessa could scarcely breathe as they crossed the foyer, expecting at any moment a heavy hand to descend on her shoulder, a liveried body to challenge them, a peaked cap to thrust into their faces. The thick carpet accused their feet. Safely inside the Ladies, she collapsed against a basin.

'Well? Isn't this better than queuing for hours? And it's free.'

'Supposing someone comes?'

'Oh stop bleating. It's perfectly all right. Daddy brought me here once – no one takes any notice of you.'

The door opened and the girls fled into cubicles and locked

the doors. After what seemed like half an hour Vanessa slid back the bolt and peeped round the door. There was Stella, bold as brass, standing at the mirror between the sleek backs of two women in stolen fur coats applying a stub of lipstick to her mouth. She washed and dried her hands and joined Stella, meeting a changed face in the glass: Stella's eyelids were smudged with green and purple, her lashes longer and darker, her skin matt with powder.

'Where did you get it?' she whispered hoarsely as the two women moved away.

'Tracy' – the friend who had lent her the stockings, with whom Vanessa, until they were safely on the train, had feared Stella would choose to go Christmas shopping instead of with her.

Women came and went and Vanessa's fear was forgotten as she applied the cosmetics to her own face.

'Now we look a bit more human,' said Stella as they surveyed themselves, Goneril and Regan, whom their own father had named Star and Butterfly. Vanessa Cardui, Painted Lady, sucked hollows into her cheeks and said, 'We really need some blusher, but it can't be helped.'

'Just a sec.'

'But Stella, it's a BAR . . . we can't . . . !'

Her alarm flooded back as Stella marched towards Edward's Bar.

'We'll get DRUNK. What about our shopping?'

Ignoring the animated temperance tract clutching her sleeve, Stella scanned the drinkers.

'Looking for someone, Miss?' the barman asked pleasantly.

'He's not here yet,' said Stella. 'Come on, Vanessa.'

She checked the coffee lounge on the way out, and as they recrossed the fearful foyer it dawned on Vanessa that Stella had planned this all along; all the way up in the train she had been expecting to find Daddy in Edward's Bar. That had been the whole point of the expedition.

*

She was afraid that Stella would turn like an injured dog and snap at her. She swallowed hard, her heart racing, as if there were words that would make everything all right, if only she could find them.

'What?' Stella did turn on her.

'He might be in Harrods.'

'Oh yes. Doing his Christmas shopping with Fergie and Di. Buying our presents.'

Vanessa might have retorted, 'The Duchess of York to you,' but she knew better than to risk the cold salt wave of misery between them engulfing the whole day. A gypsy woman barred their way with a sprig of foliage wrapped in silver.

'Lucky white heather. Bring you luck.'

'Doesn't seem to have brought you much,' snarled Stella pushing past her.

'You shouldn't have been so rude. Now she'll put a curse on us,' wailed Vanessa.

'It wasn't even real heather, dumbbell.'

'Now there's no chance we'll meet Daddy.'

Stella strode blindly past the gauntlet of people rattling tins for The Blind. Vanessa dropped in a coin and hurried after her down the steps. As they went to consult the map of the Underground they almost stumbled over a man curled up asleep on the floor, a bundle of grey rags and hair and beard tied up with string. His feet, black with dirt and disease, protruded shockingly bare into the path of the Christmas shoppers. The sisters stared, their faces chalky under their make-up.

Then a burst of laughter and singing broke out. A group of men and women waving bottles and cans were holding a private crazed party, dancing in their disfigured clothes and plastic accoutrements; a woman with long grey hair swirling out in horizontal streamers from a circlet of tinsel was clasping a young man in a close embrace as they shuffled round singing 'All I want for Christmas is my two front teeth', and he threw back his head to pour the last drops from a bottle into a toothless black hole, while their companions beat out a percussion accompaniment on bottles and cans with a braying brass of hiccups. They were the only people in that desperate and shoving crowded place who looked happy.

Stella and Vanessa were unhappy as they travelled down the escalator. The old man's feet clawed at them with broken and corroded nails; the revellers, although quite oblivious to the citizens of the other world, had frightened them; the gypsy's curse hung over them.

Harrods was horrendous. They moved bemused through the silken scented air, buffeted by headscarves, furs and green shopping bags. Fur and feathers in the Food Hall left them stupefied in the splendour of death and beauty and money.

'This is crazy,' said Stella. 'We probably couldn't afford even one quail's egg.'

Mirrors flung their scruffy reflections back at them and they half-expected to be shown the door by one of the green and gold guards and after an hour of fingering and coveting and temptation they were out in the arctic wind of Knightsbridge with two packs of Christmas cards and a round gold box of chocolate Napoleons.

In Covent Garden they caught the tail end of a piece of street theatre as a green spotted pantomime cow curvetted at them with embarrassing udders, swiping the awkward smiles off their faces with its tail. A woman dressed as a clown bopped them on the head with a balloon and thrust a bashed-in hat at them. Close up she looked fierce rather than funny. The girls paid up. It seemed that everybody in the city was engaged in a conspiracy to make them hand over their money. Two hot chocolates made another serious inroad in their finances, the size of the bill souring the floating islands of cream as they sat on white wrought-iron chairs sipping from long spoons to the accompaniment of a young man busking on a violin backed by a stereo system.

'You should've brought your cello,' said Vanessa and

choked on her chocolate as she realized she could hardly have said anything more tactless. It was He who had caused Stella's impromptu resignation from the school orchestra, leaving them in the lurch. His repetition, in front of two of His friends, of an attributed reprimand by Sir Thomas Beecham to a lady cellist had made it impossible for her to practise at home and unthinkable that she should perform on a public platform to an audience sniggering like Him, debasing her and the music.

'It's – it's not my kind of music,' she had lied miserably to Miss Philips, the music teacher.

'Well, Stella, I must say I had never thought of *you* as a disco queen,' Miss Philips had said bitterly.

Her hurt eyes strobed Stella's pale selfish face and falling-down socks as she wilted against the wall. Accusations of letting down her fellow musicians followed, and reminders of Miss Philips's struggle to obtain the cello from another school, her own budget and resources being so limited. She ignored Stella in the corridor thereafter and the pain of this was still with her, like the ominous ache in her lower abdomen. She wished she was at home curled up with a hot-water bottle.

'Bastard,' she said. 'Of all the gin joints in all the suburbs of south-east London, why did He have to walk into ours?' Mummy had brought Him home from a rehearsal of the amateur production of *Oklahoma* for which she was doing the costumes, ostensibly for an emergency fitting of His Judd Fry outfit, the trousers and boots of which were presenting difficulties. The girls had almost clapped the palms off their hands after the mournful rendition of 'Poor Judd is Dead'. It would always be a show-stopper for them.

Stella wished she had had one of the cards from Harrods to put in the school postbox for Miss Philips, but she hadn't, and now it was too late. Vanessa bought a silver heart-shaped balloon for Cordelia, or, as Stella suspected, for herself. They wandered round the stalls and shops over the slippery cobblestones glazed with drizzle.

'How come, whichever way we go, we always end up in Central Avenue?' Vanessa wondered.

Stella gave up the pretence that she knew exactly where she was going. 'It'll be getting dark soon. We must buy *something*.'

They battled their way into the Covent Garden General Store and joined the wet and unhappy throng desperate to spend money they couldn't afford on presents for people who would not want what they received, to the relentless musical threat that Santa Claus was coming to town. 'If this is more fun than just shopping,' said Stella as they queued to pay for their doubtful purchases, quoting from the notice, displayed over the festive and jokey goods, 'I think I prefer just shopping. Sainsbury's on Saturday morning is paradise compared to this.'

Stella was seduced by a gold mesh star and some baubles as fragile and iridescent as soap bubbles, to hang on the conifer in the corner of the bare front room, decked in scrawny tinsel too sparse for its sprawling branches and topped with the fairy with a scorch mark in her greying crêpe-paper skirt where it had once caught in a candle. The candles, with most of their old decorations, had been vetoed by Him and had been replaced by a set of fairy lights with more twisted emerald green flex than bulbs in evidence.

'I wish we hadn't got a tree,' Vanessa said.

'I know. Cordelia likes it, though.'

'I suppose so. That's all that matters really. I mean, Christmas *is* for kids, isn't it?'

Vanessa showed her the bubble bath disguised as a bottle of gin which she was buying for Him.

'Perhaps He'll drink it.'

'Early on Christmas morning, nursing a savage hangover, He rips open His presents and desperate for a hair-of-the-dog He puts the bottle to his lips. Bubbles come out of His nose and mouth, He falls to the floor –'

'Screaming in agony.'

'– screaming in agony, foaming at the mouth. The heroic efforts of his distraught stepdaughters fail to revive him. An ambulance is called but it gets stuck in traffic. When they finally reach the hospital all the nurses are singing carols in the wards and no one can find the stomach pump. A doctor in a paper hat tells the sorrowing sisters – or are they laughing, who can tell? – that it's too late. He has fallen victim to His own greed. How much does it cost?'

'Two pounds seventy-nine.'

'Cheap at the price.'

After leaving the shop they collided with a superstructure formed by two supermarket trolleys lashed together and heaped with a perilous pyramid of old clothes and plastic bags and utensils and bits of hardware like taps and broken car exhausts and hub-caps, the handlebars of a bicycle fronting it like antlers and three plumes of pampas grass waving in dirty Prince of Wales feathers. The owner was dragging a large cardboard box from beneath a stall of skirts and blouses.

'What do you think he wants that box for?' Vanessa wondered.

'To sleep in, of course. He probably lives in Cardboard City.'

'Cardboard City?'

'It's where the homeless people live. They all sleep in cardboard boxes underneath the Arches.'

'What arches?'

'*The* Arches, of course. Shall we go home now?'

Vanessa nodded. They were wet and cold, and the rain had removed most of their make-up, saving them the trouble of doing it themselves before they encountered Him. The feet of Stella's stockings felt like muddy string in her leaking shoes.

They were huddled on the packed escalator, two drowned rats going up to Victoria, when Vanessa screamed shrilly.

'Daddy!'

She pointed to a man on the opposing escalator.

'It's Daddy, quick Stella, we've got to get off.' She would have climbed over the rail if Stella hadn't held her.

'It's not him.'

'It is. It is. *Daddy!*'

Faces turned to stare. The man turned and their eyes met as they were carried upwards and he was borne inexorably down. Vanessa tried to turn to run down against the flow of the escalator but she was wedged. The man was gone for ever.

'It wasn't him, I tell you.' Stella fought the sobbing Vanessa at the top of the stair, they were yelling at each other in the mêlée of commuters and shoppers. She succeeded in dragging her through the barrier, still crying, 'It was him. Now we'll never see him again.'

'Daddy hasn't got a beard, you know that. And he'd never wear a balaclava. Come *on*, Vanessa, we'll miss our train.'

'It was him. Let's go back, please, please.'

'Look, stupid, that guy was a down and out. A vagrant. A wino. A meths drinker. It couldn't possibly have been Daddy.'

On the home-bound train Stella carefully opened the box of chocolate Napoleons. There were so many that nobody would notice if a couple were missing. She took out two gold coins and sealed the box again. For the rest of their lives Vanessa would be convinced that she had seen her father, and Stella would never be sure. The chocolate dissolved in their mouths as they crossed the Thames.

'Where is Cardboard City?' whispered Vanessa. 'How do you get there?'

' "Follow the Yellow Brick Road . . ." '

The silver heart-shaped balloon floated on its vertical string above the heads and newspapers of the passengers.

' "Now I know I've got a heart, because it's breaking." '

'It's just a slow puncture,' Stella said. She stuck a gift label on to the balloon's puckering silver skin. It ruined the look of it, but it was kindly meant. Vanessa looked out of the window at the moon melting like a lemon drop in the freezing sky above the chimney tops of Clapham and pictured it shining on the cold frail walls and pinnacles of Cardboard City.

'I don't want Daddy to sleep in a cardboard box,' she said.
'It's a great life,' Stella said savagely. 'Didn't you see those people singing and dancing?'

Dreams of Dead Women's Handbags

IT was a black evening bag sequined with salt, open-mouthed under a rusted marcasite clasp, revealing a black moiré silk lining stained by sea water; a relic stranded in the wrack of tarry pebbles and tufts of blue and orange nylon string like garish sea anenomes, crab shells and lobster legs, plastic detritus, oily feathers, condoms and rubbery weed and clouded glass, the dry white sponges of whelk egg cases, and a brittle black-horned mermaid's purse. This image, the wreckage of a dream beached on the morning, would not float away; as empty as an open shell, the black bivalve emitted a silent howl of despair; clouds passed through its mirror.

Like Webster, Susan Vigo was much possessed by death. Sitting on a slow train to the coast, at a table in the compartment adjacent to the buffet car, she thought about her recurring dream and about a means of murder. A book and a newspaper lay in front of her, and as she inserted the word 'limpid' in the crossword, completing the puzzle, she saw aquamarine water in a rock pool wavering limpidly over a conical white limpet shell. Her own id was rather limp that morning, she felt; the gold top of her pen tasted briny in her mouth. The colour of the water was the precise clear almost-green of spring evening skies when the city trembled with the possibility of love. She wondered dispassionately if she would ever encounter such a sky again, and as she wondered, she saw a handbag half-submerged on the bottom of the pool among the wavering weeds, green and encrusted with limpets, as though it had lain there for a long time, releasing gentle strings of bubbles like dreams and memories. A mermaid's purse, she remembered her father teaching her, as she made her way to the buffet, was the horny egg case of a skate, or ray or shark, but to whom the desolate handbag in her dreams had belonged, she had no idea, only that its owner was dead.

The buffet car steward seemed familiar, but perhaps the painful red eyes were uniform issue, along with the shiny jacket spattered by toasted sandwiches; his hair had been combed back with bacon grease and fell in curly rashers on his collar, his red tie was as slick as a dying poppy's petal. As Susan waited in the queue she told herself that he could have no possible significance in her life, and reminded herself that she made many journeys and had probably encountered him before, leering over the formica counter of another train. Nevertheless she watched him, it was her habit to stare at people, with an uneasy notion that he was Charon ferrying her across the Styx – but Charon would not be the barman, but the driver of this Inter-City train, sitting at the controls in his cab, racing them down the rails to the Elysian fields, and she was almost certain that she and her fellow passengers were still alive and their coins were for the purchase of refreshments and not the fees of the dead. The barman's years of bracing himself on the swaying floors of articulated metal snakes had given him the measure of his customers. The woman in the simulated beige mink, in front of Susan in the queue, asked for two gins and tonics, one for an imaginary friend down the corridor, and was given two little green bottles, two cans of tonic, and one plastic cup with a contemptuous fistful of ice-cubes. Her eyes met the barman's and she did not demur. One of his eyes closed like a snake's in a wink at Susan as the woman fumbled her purchases from the counter. 'It takes one to know one,' thought Susan refusing to be drawn into complicity by the reptilian lid of his red eye as she ordered her coffee. Her face in the mirror behind the bar, her shirt, her scarf, her brooch, the cut of her jacket spoke as quietly of success as the fur-coated woman's screeched failure.

Failure. That was a word Susan Vigo hated. She saw it as a sickly plant with etiolated leaves, flourishing in dank unpleasant places, a parasite on a rotting trunk, or a pot plant on the windowsills of houses of people she despised. If she had cared to, she could have supplied a net curtain on a string as a backcloth and a plaster Alsatian, but she had a horror of rotting window frames and rented rooms, and banished the image. Susan Vigo was not the sort of woman who would order two gins for herself on a train. She was not, like some she could name, the sort of writer who would arrive to give a reading with a wine-splashed book and grains of cat litter in her trouser turn-ups, having fortified herself with spirits on the journey for the ordeal, who would enter in disarray and stumble into disrepute. The books in her overnight bag were glossy and immaculate with clean white strips of paper placed between the pages, to mark the passages which she would read. She did not regard it as an ordeal; she had memorized her introductory speech, and was looking forward to the evening. She had done her homework, and would have been able to relax with a book by another author had consciousness of the delivery date of her own next crime novel not threatened like a migraine at the edge of her brain. The irony was that the title of her book was *Deadline* and for the first time in her life, she feared that she would not meet hers. Notice of it had appeared already in her publisher's catalogue and she had not even got the plot. It was set on the coast, she knew that; it involved a writer – yes, and horned poppy and sea holly and viper's bugloss, stranded sea-mice leaking rainbows into the sand, and of course her Detective Inspector Christopher Hartshorn, an investigator of the intellectual, laconic school; a body –

naturally; a handbag washed up on the beach – the sort of handbag that had foxtrotted to Harry Roy, or a flaunting scarlet patent number blatant as a stiletto heel, a steel-faceted purse, a gondola basket holding a copy of *Mirabelle* or *Roxy* – she didn't even know in which period to set her murder – a drawstring leather bag which smelled of raw camel hide, a satchel with a wooden pencil box, a strap purse, containing a threepenny bit, worn across the front of a gymslip – old handbags like discarded lovers. She sifted desperately through the heap of silk and plastic, leather and wicker – it had to be black, like the handbag in her dream . . .

Susan lived in Hampstead, on a staple diet of vodka and asparagus, fresh in season, or tinned. It made life simple; she never had to think about what food to buy except when she had guests, which was not very often; she was more entertained than entertaining. She loved her flat and lived there alone. She had once been given two love-birds but had grown jealous of their absorption in each other and had given them away. Trailing plants now entwined the bars of the cage where the pink and yellow birds had preened, kissing each other with waxy bills; she preferred their green indifference. There was not a trace of a plaster Alsatian. The man who had seduced her had introduced her to asparagus, its tender green heads swimming in butter, with baked beans – her choice. Professor Bruno Rosenblum, lecturer in poetry who although his juxtaposed names conjured up withered roses on their stems, had once strewn the bed with roses while she slept. Waking in the scent and petals, she had wept. ' "Ah, as the heart grows older, it will come to such sights colder," ' she thought now, in the train, remembering, as the past, like the dried petals of pot-pourri exhaled a slight sad scent, and 'Perhaps G.M. Hopkins got it right – it is always ourselves for whom we are grieving – enough of this' she turned from the dirty window slashed with rain that obscured the flat landscape and the dun animals in the shabby February fields, to her book. She wondered if she could, perhaps, take its central situation or *donnée*, and by changing it subtly, and substituting her own characters, manufacture a convincingly original work . . .

' "If you want to know about a woman, look in her purse." ' The detective dumped the clues to the dead dame's life into a plastic bag and consigned it to Forensic. Susan's own handbag, if studied, would have told of an orderly life and mind, or of an owner who had dumped all her old make-up in the bin and dashed into an expensive chemist's on the way to the station: no sleazy clutter there, no circle of foam rubber tinged with grimy powder, no sweating stubs of lipstick and broken biros leaking into the lining, or tobacco shreds or dog-eared appointment cards for special clinics or combs with dirty teeth or minicab cards acquired on flights through dawn streets from unspeakable crises. Susan could see as clearly in her mind the contents of the handbag of the woman who had bought the two gins as she could see her black stilettos resting on the next seat, and the fall of fake fur caressing her calf. She saw her lean forward and open a compact the dark blue of a mussel shell, and peer into a mirror, and her imagination supplied a crack zigzagging across the glass, presaging doom. The man directly opposite Susan was reading a report and was of as little interest as he had been at the start of the journey; on the other side of the aisle a family, parents and two children, finished their enormous lunch and settled down to a game of three-dimensional noughts and crosses, which involved plastic tubes and marbles, clack clack clack. The marbles bounced off Susan's brain like bullets. 'Why can't they just use pencil and paper?' she thought irritably: the extra dimensions added nothing but cost and noise to the game. She put her hands over her ears, and, resting her book on the table, tried to read, but her concentration was shot to pieces. She closed her eyes, and the handbag in her dream returned like a black shell, which if held to the ear would whisper her own mortality.

There was this handbag washed up on the beach – what next? She waited for a whole narrative to unwind and a cast of characters to come trooping out, but nothing happened. There was this crime writer travelling on a train, panicking about a deadline when suddenly . . . a single shot passed through the head of the buffet car attendant's head, shattering the glass behind him . . . Susan's fascination with firearms dated from a white double holster studded with glass jewels and two fancy guns with bluish shining barrels and decorated stocks; she had loved them more than any of her dolls, taking them to bed with her at night, loving the neat round boxes of pink caps. She could smell them now, and the scent of new sandals with crêpe soles like cheese.

Dreams of dead women's handbags: the click of a false tortoiseshell clasp, the musty smell of old perfume from the torn black moiré lining, and powder in a shell, lipstick that would look as ghastly on a skull as it did on the mouths of the little white flat fish on the seaside stall, skate smoking cigarettes through painted mouths, the glitter of saliva on a pin impaling whelks. She saw a man and a woman walking on a cliff top starred with pink thrift, a seagull's white scalloped tail feathers; the woman wore a dress patterned in poppies and corn and the man had his shirt-collar open over his jacket, in holiday style. A child skipped between them on that salty afternoon when the world was their oyster.

Amberley Hall, where Susan was heading, was a small private literary foundation where students of all ages attended courses and summer schools in music, painting and writing. She had been invited to be the guest reader at one of their creative writing courses, and was looking forward to seeing again the two tutors, both friends, and renewing her acquaintance with Amberley's directors whom she had liked very much when she met them the previous year when she herself had been a co-tutor. The house was white and stood on a cliff; reflections of the sea and sky met in its windows. Susan hoped that she would be given the room in which she had slept before, with its faded blue bedspread and shell-framed looking-glass and vase of dried flowers beside the white shells on the windowsill, sea lavender faded by time, like a dead woman's passions and regrets. The clatter of marbles became intolerable. Susan strode towards the buffet car. The train seemed to be going very slowly. She began to worry about the time and wish that she had accepted her hosts's offer to meet her at the station.

'Going all the way?' the barman asked as he sliced a lemon with a thin-bladed knife. The other woman had not been offered lemon.

'I beg your pardon?'

'Going all the way?'

'No. Not quite.'

'Business or pleasure?'

Susan had never seen why she should answer that question, so often asked by strangers on a train.

'A bit of both,' she replied.

Again his eyelid flickered in a wink.

'Ice?'

'Please.' She hoped her tone matched the cubes he was dropping into her glass with his fingers, one of which was girdled with a frayed plaster. Stubble was trying to break through the red nodules of a rash on his neck; he looked as though he had shaved in cold water in the basin in the blocked toilet, with his knife. The arrival of two other customers brought their conversation to an end.

As she approached her seat with her vodka and tonic she stopped in her tracks. That woman in the fur coat had Susan's overnight bag down on the seat and was going through her things.

'What do you think you're doing?' She grabbed her furry arm; her hand was shaken from it.

'I'm just looking for a tissue.'

'But that's my bag. Those are my things!'

The woman was pulling out clothes and underclothes and dumping them on the seat while the noughts and crosses clicked and clacked, tic tac toe. She scrabbled under the books at the bottom of the bag.

'Stop it, do you hear?'

'She's only looking for a tissue,' said the man opposite mildly, looking up from his report.

'I'm going to get the guard. I'm going to pull the emergency cord.'

The other woman's full lips shook and she started to cry.

The man took a handkerchief from his breast pocket, shook it out and handed it to her.

'Have a good blow.'

She did.

'I'll give you a good blow!' said Susan punching her hard in the chest, at the top of a creased *décolletage* where a gilt pendant nestled in the shape of the letter M. The lights went out. The train almost concertinaed to a stop.

'Now look what you've done, pulling the communication cord.'

'I didn't touch it,' Susan shouted. 'What's going on? What's the matter with everybody? I didn't go near it.'

She felt the woman move away, and sat down heavily on her disarranged bag, panting with affront and rage, the unfairness of it all and the fact that nobody had stood up for her. Tears were rolling down her face as she groped for her clothes and crammed them back into the bag. Marbles rolled across the table and ricocheted off the floor. The tips of cigarettes glowed like tiny volcanoes in the gloom and someone giggled, a high nervous whinny. Susan began to sweat. Rain was drumming on the windows like her heart-beats, and she knew that she had died and was to be locked for eternity in this train in the dark with people who hated her. This was her sentence: what was her crime? Battalions of minor sins thronged her memory. Her hand hurt where she had punched the woman; she sucked her knuckle and tasted blood. The lights came on. Susan screamed.

The barman stood in the doorway, his knife in his hand.

'Nearly a nasty accident,' he said. 'Car stalled on the level crossing.'

People started to laugh and talk.

'Could've been curtains for us all,' he said as the train brayed and the orange curtains at the black windows swayed as it started to move.

The woman in the fur coat came sashaying down the aisle, reeled on a marble, and plonked herself down beside Susan.

'Sorry about that little mistake, only I mistook it for my bag. They're quite similar. Here, let me help you put it up.'

They swung it clumsily onto the rack, next to a dirty tapestry bag edged in cracked vinyl. Susan looked into her eyes, opaque as marbles, and perceived that she was mad. She picked up her book.

'Like reading, do you?'

'When I get the chance.'

'I know what you mean. There's always something needs doing, isn't there? I expect you're like me, can't sit idle. What with my little dog, and my crochering and the telly there's always something, isn't there?'

'Crochering?' Susan heard herself ask.

'Yes, I've always got some on the go. I made this.'

She pulled open her lapels to show a deep-throated pink filigree garment.

'It was a bolero in the pattern, only I added the sleeves.'

Susan smiled and tried desperately to read, but it was too late: she saw in vivid detail the woman's sitting room, feet in pink fluffy slippers stretched out to the electric fire that was mottling her legs, the wheezy Yorkshire terrier with a growth on its neck, the crochet hook plying in a billowy sea of pink and violet squares; a bedspread for a wedding present to a niece, who would bundle it into a cupboard.

She almost said, 'I'm sorry about your little dog,' but stopped herself in time, and before she was tempted to advise her to abandon her bedspread, the guard announced that the train was approaching her station. She gathered her things together with relief and went to find an exit. As she passed the bar the steward, who had taken off his jacket and was reading a newspaper, did not raise his head. She saw how foolish she had been to fear him.

'Thank God that's over,' she said aloud on the platform as she took deep breaths of wet dark air which although the station was miles inland, tasted salty, and the appalling train pulled away, carrying the barman and the deranged woman to their mad destinations. She came out into the forecourt in time to see the rear lights of a taxi flashing in the rain. She knew at once that it was the only one and that it would not return for a long time. She saw a telephone box across the road, and shielding with her bag her hair that the rain would reduce to a nest of snakes hurried through the puddles. At least, being in the country, the phone would not have been vandalized. A wet chip paper wrapped itself round her ankles; the receiver dangled from a mess of wires, black with emptiness roaring through its broken mouth, like a washed-up handbag.

A pub. There must be a pub somewhere near the station that would have a telephone. Susan stepped out of the smell of rural urine and started to walk. She would not let herself panic, or let the lit and curtained windows sheltering domesticity make her feel lonely. Perhaps she could hire a car, from the pub. She imagined the sudden silence falling on the jocular company of the inn and a fearful peasant declaring, 'None of us villagers dare go up to Amberley Hall. Not after dark,' and a dark figure in a bat-winged cloak flying screeching past the moon.

Mine host was a gloomy fellow who pointed her to a pay phone. The number was engaged. Temporarily defeated, Susan ordered a drink and sat down. It was then that she realized that her overnight bag had been transformed into a grubby tapestry hold-all with splitting vinyl trim. A cold deluge of disbelief engulfed her and then hot pricking needles of anger. She drowned the words that rose to her lips; this wasn't Hampstead. How could it have happened – that madwoman – Susan was furious with herself; she would have scorned to use the device of the switched luggage in one of her own books, and here she was, lumbered, in this dire pub, with this disgusting bag, and worse, worse, all her own things, her books – the reading . . . She was tempted to call it a day then, and order another drink, and consign herself to fate, propping up the bar until her money ran out and they dumped her in the street, but she made another attempt at the telephone, and this time got through. Someone would be there to pick her up in twenty minutes. She thought of ordering a sandwich but the knowledge of the meal, the refectory table heaped with bowls of food awaiting her, restrained her, and she sat there half listening to the juke-box, making her drink last, wishing she was at home doing something cheerful like drinking vodka and listening to Bessie Smith, or Billie Holiday singing 'Good Morning Heartache'.

She thought she had found her murder victim, a blonde woman with a soft white face and body and a pendant in the shape of the letter M and a stolen bag; she lolled in death, her black shoes stabbing skywards, on a cliff top lying in the thrift that starred the grass and was embossed on a threepenny bit, tarnished at the bottom of an old handbag. Threepence, that was the amount of pocket money she had received; a golden hexagonal coin each Saturday morning. The early 1950s: a dazzle of red, white and blue; father, mother and child silhouetted against a golden sunburst in a red sky like figures on a poster, marching into Utopia.

The dead woman's dress was splashed with poppies and corn – no, that was wrong – it must be black. Her mother had had a dress of poppies and corn, scarlet flowers and golden ears and sky-blue cornflowers on a white field; Ceres in white peep-toe shoes, the sun sparkling off a Kirbigrip in her dark gold hair. Her father's hair was bright with brilliantine and he wore his shirt-collar, white as vanilla ice cream, open over his jacket. Susan's hair was in two thin plaits of corn and gripped on either side with a white hair-slide in the shape of Brumas the famous polar bear cub. Susan sat in the pub, becoming aware that it was actually a small hotel and staring at a red-carpeted staircase that disappeared at an angle, leading to the upper guest rooms. In a flash she realized why the barman in the train looked familiar, and blind and deaf to the music and flashing lights she sat in a waking dream.

The child woke in the hotel bedroom and found herself alone. Moonlight lay on the pillows of the double bed her parents shared. The bed was undisturbed. They had come up from the bar to tuck her in. 'You be a good girl now and go to sleep. We're just popping out for a stroll, we won't be gone more than a few minutes.' Her father's eyes were red – she turned her face away from his beery kiss. Her mother's best black taffeta dress rustled as she closed the door behind them. She pulled a sweater over her nightdress and buckled on her holster and her new white sandals and tiptoed to the door. A gust of piano playing and singing and beer and cigarette smoke bellied into the bedroom. She closed the door quietly behind her and slid slowly down the banister, so as not to make any noise. She was angry with them for leaving her alone. She bet they were eating ice creams and chips without her. She crept to the back door and let herself out into the street. Although she had never been out so late alone, she found that it was almost light – girls and boys come out to play, the moon doth shine as bright as day – she would burst into the café and shoot them dead – Susan saw her in the moonlight, a small figure in a white nightdress in the empty street with a gun in each hand. The café was closed.

She turned on to the path that led to the cliffs. Rough grass spiked her bare legs and sand filled her new sandals and rubbed on her heels. She holstered her guns because she had to use her hands to scramble up the steep slope, uttering little sobs of fear and rage. She reached the top and flung herself panting on to the turf. At the edge of the cliff sat two figures, from this distance as black as two cormorants on a rock against the sky. The sea was roaring in her ears as she wriggled on her belly towards them. As she drew nearer she could see the woman's arms, white as vanilla in her black taffeta dress and the man's shirt-collar. She stood up and drew her guns and took aim but suddenly she was frightened at herself standing there against the sky and just wanted them to hold her, and shoved the guns back in the holster and as she did the man put his arm round the woman's shoulder and kissed her. The child was running towards them, to thrust herself between their bodies shouting joyfully 'Boo!' as she thumped them on their backs and the woman lost her balance and clutched the man and they went tumbling over and over and over and the woman's handbag fell from her wrist and went spiralling after them screaming and screaming from its open black mouth.

When the landlady, impatient at the congealing breakfast, came to rouse the family in the morning she found the child asleep, cuddled up to a holster instead of a teddy. The parents' bed was undisturbed. It seemed a shame to wake the little girl. She looked so peaceful with her fair hair spread out on the pillow. She shook her gently.

'Where are your mummy and daddy, lovey?'

The child sat up, seeing the buckle of her new sandal hanging by a thread. Mummy would have to sew it on.

'I don't know,' she answered truthfully.

'Susan. Hi.' Tom from Amberley Hall was shaking her arm. 'You look awful. Have you had a terrible journey? You must have.'

'Perfectly bloody,' said Susan.

'I'm afraid you've missed supper,' said Tom, in the car, 'but we'll rustle up something for you after the reading. I think we'd better get straight on with it if you don't mind. Everybody's keen to meet you. Quite an interesting bunch of students this time . . .'

His voice went on. Susan wanted to bury her face in the thick cables of his sweater. As they entered the house she explained about the loss of her bag.

'Just like Professor Pnin, eh, on the wrong train with the wrong lecture?' he laughed. Susan wished then profoundly to be Professor Pnin, Russian and ideally bald; to be anybody but herself in her creased clothes with her hair snaking wildly round her head and a tapestry bag in her hand containing the crocheted tangle of that woman's mad life.

'It was the right train,' she said, 'but I haven't got anything to read.'

'I did get in touch with your publishers to send some books to sell, but I'm afraid they haven't arrived. Never mind though, some of the students have brought their own copies for you to sign so you could borrow one. Five minutes to freshen up, OK? We've put you in the same room as last time.'

'No bloody food. No bloody wine. Not even any bloody books,' said Susan behind the closed door of her room. She aimed a kick at the bookcase: each of those spines faded by sea air representing somebody's futile bid to hold back eternal night. Precisely five minutes later she stepped, pale, poised and professional, into the firelit room to enchant her audience.

When she had finished reading, a chill hung over the room for a moment and then someone started the clapping. As the appreciative applause flickered out, bottles of wine and glasses were brought, and the evening was given over to informal questions and discussion. A gallant in corduroys bowed as he handed her a glass.

'You're obviously very successful, Miss Vigo, or may I call you Susan? Could you tell us what made you decide on writing as a career in the first place? I mean I myself have been attempting to –'

'I wanted to be rich,' interrupted Susan quickly before he could launch on his autobiography. The firelight striking red glints on her hair, and her charming smile persuaded her listeners that she was joking. 'You see, I was always determined to succeed in whatever career I chose. I came from a very deprived background. My parents died tragically when I was young and I was brought up by relatives.' Her lip trembled slightly; a plaster Alsatian barked in corroboration.

'What was your first big breakthrough?'

'I was very lucky in that I met a professor at university, a dear old soul, who took an interest in my youthful efforts and who was very helpful to me professionally. He's dead now, alas.' She became for a moment a pretty young student paying grateful tribute to her crusty old mentor. Most of the audience were half in love with her now.

'What made you turn to crime, as it were, Susan, instead of to any other fictional form?'

Susan's slender body rippled as she giggled, 'I don't know really – I developed a taste for murder at an early age, and I've never looked back, I suppose.'

'Can I ask where you get your ideas from?'

The frail orphan sipped her wine before replying.

'From "the foul rag-and-bone shop of the heart".'

Perpetual Spinach

OLD Cartwright belonged to the snow-shovelling generation. The dread sound of metal scraping the pavement woke his young neighbours and even before they were aware of the strange feathery light in the bedroom they knew it was snowing, and pictured him holding out his spade to catch the first sparse flakes falling from the sky. They groaned at the thought of that old man shovelling their shared path, as he surely would, and pulled the duvet over their heads, burying themselves in goose feathers.

Despite his London ancestry there was something bucolic about Old Cartwright; a sense of warm rabbits dangling from his belt, or a brace of wood-pigeons with rubies of blood on their breasts. He rode a stiff old black woman's bicycle to his urban allotment, pedalling slowly with one corduroy trouser leg, the colour of ploughed fields, caught up in a cycle clip and the other tied up with string. The bicycle, like its owner Miss Defreitas, his sub-tenant, who lived above Mr Cartwright, was old and stiff and black, and was furnished with wicker baskets front and rear in which he brought back bouquets of carrots, potatoes and beans, frilly dark savoy cabbages, rhubarb and, endlessly, spinach. 'I can see why it's called perpetual spinach,' Olivia had said despairingly, plunging her hands into yet another washing-up bowl full of wet leaves. He set traps of jam jars filled with beer for the slugs and snails and they floundered and drowned, swelling to grotesque bleached alcoholic fungi before he threw them in a jellied heap on the compost. His crops were nourished on blood and bonemeal; the veins of his beetroots ran red above their swollen globes, his tomatoes were solid balls of haemoglobin and under their toxic green umbrellas the sanguineous sticks of his rhubarb were as thick as vulture's legs. Until his retirement he had been a driver on the Southern Region of British Rail, and Miss Defreitas had cleaned trains. She had been one of those women whose dustpan and brush were as much a reproach to commuters, swinging their feet out of the path of the cartons and cups and cigarette butts left by their predecessors, in the guilty knowledge that they would be replacing the rubbish as soon as she had gone, as Old Cartwright's spade was to Nick and Olivia. Miss Defreitas received his vegetables with politeness, although she continued to buy sweet potatoes and other strange tubers and roots which he could not identify, and refused to try. At first, Nick and Olivia had indulged in lewd speculation about the relationship of their elderly neighbours, but apart from Sunday lunch, which they took turns to cook, when Old Cartwright returned from the pub and Miss Defreitas from church, and the occasional sultry evenings when she brought out a kitchen chair and sat fanning herself while he slopped water over the begonias in the bed at the side of the yard, they led separate lives.

'This is ridiculous,' Nick said, hobbling to the window wrapped in the duvet, leaving Olivia exposed on the bed. 'Doesn't he know that if you clear the snow from outside your house you are responsible if anybody slips and breaks a leg?' He banged on the window and shouted at Cartwright to put back their snow. The double glazing muffled his voice and Old Cartwright, looking up with dimmed eyes, perceived him to be wearing an off-the-shoulder ball gown and raised his spade in an old-soldierly salute.

'If this keeps on, we can build a snowman later,' said Olivia.

'Dress it up in one of Old Cartwright's caps and pelt it with snowballs,' agreed Nick coming back to bed. The radio came on and he pressed the snooze button.

'Why do those old fogeys have to get up so early?'

'Because they haven't anything better to do,' Olivia snuggled into him.

Why despite the earthy bundles of produce left on their doorstep, Nick and Olivia sometimes wondered, did they regard him as a horrible old man? True, they had once heard him braying through the fence in mockery of the laughter at one of their parties where the guests spilled into the yard on summer nights, and one of their friends had asked if there was a donkey next door. She was pissed, of course; they all were. 'Only a silly ass,' Nick had replied quick as a flash; it was hilarious, but generally Cartwright was no trouble. They did not know about the slugs and snails, having resisted his invitations to visit the allotment, but taking the grisly titbits suspended from his washing line for the birds as an indication, fantasized a gamekeeper's gibbet of crucified fur and feathers on his tool-shed wall. Before they had learned that he had been a train driver they had decided that he was a ratcatcher. There was an empty rabbit hutch by his back door, mossy-roofed, with wire netting rusted to brittleness. At their firework party, Miss Defreitas had appeared at her window as a floating white nightdress against the blackness. Olivia held out a sparkler to her but a rocket whizzing toward the house made her disappear in a burst of golden stars, leaving the midnight sky and her window darker than before.

'Stupid old cockroach,' Nick had said, but Olivia had been pleased that their youthful pyrotechnics had lighted up her drab life for a minute or two.

'You ought to get yourself an allotment,' Old Cartwright had told Nick, leaning over the wooden fence that separated their back yards. It was broken, pulled down or held in the arms of an old Russian vine, and was, as he was fond of pointing out, their responsibility. 'Keep the missis in fruit and veg. I'll have a word with my committee. There's a waiting list, but a word in the right ear . . .'

He rubbed his own right lobe between an earthy finger and thumb while the thin burned-out cigarette stuck to his lip waggled in complicity.

'I wouldn't have time to look after an allotment,' Nick responded in weak alarm from the lounger where he lay with a book and a pitcher of Pimms, swiping at a wasp as if warding off a barrage of onions and tomatoes. He swung his legs, still golden from a Turkish holiday, in cut-off denim shorts, to the ground and took refuge in the kitchen, leaving the Pimms, like one of Cartwright's traps, to entice a variety of winged insects to a sweet and sticky death among the mint and melting ice floes.

'Oh, you've just broken my dream,' Olivia said, when he told her. 'I had a really funny dream last night. Henry was on a bicycle going to the allotments. When I say funny, it wasn't really funny, it was scary for some reason; I can't remember . . .' Henry cycled across her consciousness, his tabby trousers encircled with a bicycle clip and a piece of string, and the image faded.

'Look – he's got earth in his pads! That proves . . .'

'Been scratching in the begonias next door.'

'I suppose so.'

As she put down the food for Henry and his black companion Ruby, she thought for a second that a thin burned-out cigarette stuck from his mouth, but it turned out, to her relief, to be a tiny white feather.

It had been in a summer smelling of basil and tomatoes that they had moved into one of the row of pretty artisan's dwellings, some still hung like the cottage next door with net curtains and others with the coloured rattan and bamboo blinds of *arrivistes*, such as themselves. Old Cartwright had occupied his house for sixty years; Nick and Olivia, who intended to remain in theirs for not more than two or three, were shocked by the way he had let his property deteriorate. It looked doubly disreputable beside their repointed brickwork and fresh paint; Miss Defreitas had geraniums in white plastic pots on her front windowsill and there was even a gnome and a stone tortoise in the tiny front garden. One night Nick and Olivia had attached a piece of battered cod from the chip shop to the end of the gnome's fishing rod, but one of their cats had eaten it before morning and spoiled the joke; and their plan to replace the stone reptile with a live one had been thwarted so far by the import ban on tortoises. They had a special loathing of the curtain of coloured plastic strips that hung across the open back door in summer.

'Makes it look like a betting shop,' grumbled Nick to their closest friends Annabel and Mark, as they set up the barbecue.

'If there's a chance of it ever coming on the market,' Mark said, 'we want to be the first to know.'

'That would be brilliant,' sighed Olivia.

'Do they use that old tin bath?' asked Annabel pointing to the thing hanging from a nail on the outside wall.

'Not any more,' said Nick.

'We shall use it,' Mark said, 'in front of the kitchen fire. Annabel can scrub my back when I come off shift at t'pit.'

'Brilliant. Very D.H. Lawrence.' They laughed as sparks flew like fireflies and the smell of grilled flesh made their mouths water and the cats came crashing over the fence. It was such a lovely evening that it was three o'clock before the last meaty and winey kisses were exchanged and the last goodbyes shouted into the sleeping street and the last car door banged.

In the morning Old Cartwright complained to Olivia that the cats had broken one of his begonias. She reported it to Nick, adding, 'I'm never sure whether I like begonias or not. I can't decide if they are beautiful or obscene.'

'Need one preclude the other?'

'They're like roses but too fleshy – if he didn't plant them so regularly., so far apart, with all that bald earth in between, they might look better . . . anyway, he accused the cats of breaking one.'

'Did they?'

'Mmm. I denied it of course. How pathetic, one measly flower . . .'

'You'd think Miss Defreitas might run to something more exotic. I mean, begonias and geraniums in plastic pots – some bougainvillaea or mimosa – a bit of tropical splendour –'

'I don't think Martinique is in the tropics.'

'– the brilliant hues of hummingbirds darting through the frangipani, the flash of a hyacinthine macaw's wing reflecting the waters of a blue lagoon . . .'

'You'd like a hummingbird, wouldn't you?' Olivia seized the black cat, Ruby, and kissed her nose. 'Or a hyacinthine wing . . . that's funny, Nick, Ruby smells of perfume . . . it's not mine, sort of sickly, and cheap . . . I wonder what she's been up to?'

'All cats lead secret lives their owners know nothing about. Have you any idea where Henry goes at night?'

'No, but I wish he'd stay in.'

'She's not very good value, is she, our Miss Defreitas? I mean, remember when we peeked into her church and she was just standing there, in her pink hat, singing a hymn, not flinging herself around, rolling her eyes and waving her hands in the air and shouting "Hallelujah, yes Lord, I'se a comin'!" and speaking in tongues. She really ought to make more effort.'

Ruby leapt from Olivia's arms, scratching her shoulder.

Summer seemed far away as Monday morning's cold-chisel broke the lover's embrace and they, having decided to leave their cars at home, set out to walk to the station. 'Here comes the Green Wellie Brigade,' said Old Cartwright as they passed.

'Boring old f—,' Nick started saying and ended in a bellow

as Olivia rubbed a cold handful of snow down his neck. The snow exhilarated her; she felt as frisky as a young husky in harness.

'Do you think we'll have a white Christmas, Mr Cartwright?' she called, knowing how he loved to expound weather lore. He looked up at the sky.

'Plenty more where that came from,' he pronounced, 'but it'll all be gone in a couple of days.'

'Why bother to shovel it up then?' asked Nick, rubbing the back of his neck with his scarf. 'Hope you fall and break your leg,' he muttered, as Miss Defreitas came out of the front door with a mug of something steaming. 'What a pair.'

That evening there was a ring at the front door. Annabel answered it, as Nick and Olivia were busy in the kitchen.

'There's a funny old man at the door,' she called, coming into the kitchen. 'I think it might be your next-door neighbour. Something about calor gas . . .'

Old Cartwright stood, stamping his feet on the step, in overcoat and gloves letting a current of icy air into the hall. Nick noticed his nose was cross-hatched with red veins with a dewdrop threatening to fall. He was asking Nick to drive him and an empty gas cylinder to the hardware shop in the morning.

'They was supposed to deliver Wednesday, only they never came,' he explained. 'I wouldn't ask, only . . . nice and warm in here, innit? Normally I wouldn't ask, only . . .'

'Oh, all right,' Nick cut him off. 'It'll have to be early. I've got a meeting at ten. It's very inconvenient.'

'Bloody liberty,' he said, when he had got rid of Cartwright. 'I hope he doesn't think I'm going to make a habit of chauffeuring him all over the place.' He had to send Cartwright back into the house in the morning to get an old blanket to wrap the cylinder in so that it would not damage the car; the thing weighed a ton even when empty. The house was as cold as it was outside, he noticed when he rolled the new cylinder over the doorstep. Miss Defreitas leaned over the banister in her black coat.

'This place is like an icebox,' he told them. 'You ought to get in touch with the council, or somebody, get some double glazing and draught proofing.' Soggy newspaper was wedged round the windows.

Nick and Olivia spent Christmas with Olivia's parents near Godalming. True to Old Cartwright's prediction it was not white, but simulated snow drifted in the leaded window panes and the porch was picked out in frosted fairy lights and the old cedar tree in the front garden was hung with coloured bulbs. The only fly in the ointment, or mulled wine, for Olivia and Nick, was that they had had to ask Old Cartwright and Miss Defreitas to feed the cats, and from time to time, scratching the heads of Olivia's parents' Jack Russell and hyperactive Red Setter, they wondered how they were getting on.

They let themselves in to their own house to find a brown skeleton of a Christmas tree, like an ancient murdered princess still wearing her jewels, surrounded by a circle of needles. There was no thud of flying feet to greet them, no loud welcoming purring, not even the swish of a resentful tail.

'Ruby, Henry,' called Olivia from the back door. Miss Defreitas appeared silhouetted against an upstairs window, and Old Cartwright poked his head out of the back door. Olivia shut her door quickly. Nick was inspecting the cupboard. He brought out several tins of cat food.

'They haven't been feeding them,' Olivia shrieked. 'They must have starved to death! Oh Nick, where are they?'

'Don't panic. Don't cry, they'll be around somewhere, hang on, the pilchards have gone, and the salmon for their Christmas dinner – and the cod in cheese and butter sauce have gone from the fridge . . . they can't have starved. They're punishing us for going away – you know what cats are like, they'll turn up at supper time, large as life. You sit down, I'll make a cup of tea.'

'Don't you think it's odd,' Olivia asked as they sat in the kitchen, relieved to have their hands round their familiar mugs of tea, 'that those particular items should have gone?'

'If you're thinking what I think you are, I'm sure cat food would be more to our neighbour's taste – Whiskas and two veg, followed by rhubarb and custard.'

When Olivia had cooked rhubarb according to Old Cartwright's instructions, with no water and a spoonful of strawberry jam, she had had to throw away the pan, one of a set, a wedding present. She, as the rhubarb had done, still seethed at the memory. The cat-flap banged and Henry and Ruby stalked in, tails in the air.

'They're enormous! They must have put on a stone! What on earth have they been feeding them on?'

'Curried goat? Yams? Perpetual spinach?'

'Whatever, they look marvellous. Come on then pussies, have you missed your mummy then?'

The two cats walked straight past them and into the bedroom. Nick and Olivia had to laugh, they looked so disdainful.

'Shouldn't we go next door and thank them?'

'Tomorrow will do – let's go to bed. I find Godalming somewhat inhibiting.'

'I noticed. Do you think we should have brought them something?'

'I thought you put some bits of turkey in a bag?'

'Old Cartwright and Miss Defreitas, silly, not the cats.'

'They loved looking after them. Gave them something to do, poor old things. Give them the turkey if you like, of course . . .'

'No, it's for the cats.'

They went to bed. The cats leapt on and walked, purring, all over them.

'Ouch. Ruby, delighted as I am to see you, do you mind not sitting on my face?'

'Yuk, Henry absolutely stinks of cigarette smoke. Mind your claws!'

'I suppose they're just pleased to see us – ouch, get off. This is ridiculous. Go and eat your nice turkey.' He pushed the cats off the bed. 'That's better. Oh God, I didn't mean bring it in here to eat – they're dragging it all over the bed, it's disgusting. Get off! What's the matter with them?'

The cats tore the meat with teeth and claws, purring and chewing simultaneously; their eyes were huge and yellow. Olivia and Nick lay there, under their weight, almost afraid to shoo them off, waiting for them to finish. Then they started to wash; the bed throbbed with their snouting and licking; it seemed they would never finish; they must have swelled to the size of tigers as their tongues rasped vast tracts of fur, licking their own and each other's enormous limbs and backs and faces, slicking paws across great ears, with whiskers rattling like embattled porcupines' quills. At last they decided to sleep, one on either side of Nick and Olivia, pulling the duvet taut across them, weighing it down so that the two humans lay side by side, swaddled like mummies, slick with sweat, unable to turn or move their restless legs, pinioned in misery all the intolerable night.

In the morning the cats resumed their normal size and seemed to be their old selves, except for the fact that Ruby never quite lost the smell of perfume and Henry's coat still reeked of tobacco smoke. Olivia and Nick got out of the way of encouraging them to jump on to their knees, although they would have said they were as fond of them as ever. They kept meaning to go round and thank their neighbours for feeding them, but they kept putting it off, and then it seemed too late. Life went on as before. Old Cartwright cycled to the allotment when the weather wasn't too bad to tend his winter and early spring greens; the wing mirror was ripped off one of the cars, and the radio stolen. Olivia and Nick entertained friends and went to the cinema and restaurants, the fence sagged and bits broke off as the cats came and went, aconites appeared in the front garden; Miss Defreitas gave them a reproachful good morning as she stepped aside in the sound of church bells to let them pass her on the path with their heavy cartons from the Wine Warehouse.

One Saturday morning in April Annabel and Mark came over. Mark and Nick were in the front room fortifying themselves before attempting to mend the fence, standing at the window with glasses in their hands. The cats were sprawled on the path luxuriating in the dust and sun on their fur. Down the road Nick saw Old Cartwright pedalling homewards, encounter Miss Defreitas coming out of the shop, and dismount. He took her shopping bag and hung it from his handlebars. She was carrying a fan of unripe bananas, bright green against her black coat. They approached the zebra-crossing.

'Don't you worry about them, with that dangerous road?' Mark said, meaning the cats. Nick was watching Old Cartwright and Miss Defreitas and misunderstood.

'Oh, they're indestructible. Besides, they always use the crossing.'

As he spoke a lorry slewed across the zebra, hurling Miss Defreitas and Old Cartwright in an arc of bodies, bicycle and bananas that was suspended in the air, then came crashing in a blitz of vegetables into the protective grille on the off-licence window, bounced, and fell in a twisted heap to the pavement.

Witnessing the accident knocked Nick for six. Both he and Olivia were surprised at how the accident affected them. Nobody could eat lunch. The policemen who came to interview Nick and Mark found the four of them holding a wake, sitting stunned and tear-stained round the kitchen table heaped with the empty bottles and full ashtrays of the bereaved. It took the officers some time to convince the mourners that Old Cartwright and Miss Defreitas had not been killed, but were in hospital, mangled like the bicycle, critically ill but still alive. The bicycle itself was a write-off. Olivia and Annabel rushed off to the newsagent's to buy Get Well cards; they found the perfect one for Old Cartwright, a still life of fruit and vegetables, and a lovely one for Miss Defreitas, with white lilies, that said 'With Deepest Sympathy', that they were sure would be to her taste.

Then they realized that they didn't know where to send the cards. Nick said he would ring the local hospital to enquire but was informed that there was no casualty department there and before he could ask where the nearest one was the phone was put down.

'Yellow Pages,' said Mark.

'Local Thomson's Directory,' suggested Annabel.

'That's the one sponsored by that ghastly cat in a T-shirt, with no trousers, isn't it?' said Olivia, but in the event they couldn't find the directories, which Olivia had forgotten she had pushed under the bed when they were repapering the bedroom. The quartet spent the rest of the day in a subdued game of Trivial Pursuit, and later the girls made some toast and pâté. Nick was sick.

The local paper gave a graphic account of the accident to the two pensioners and said that a court case was pending but did not name the hospital to which the victims had been taken. The cards grew dusty on the mantelpiece. Olivia realized that 'With Deepest Sympathy' was perhaps not suitable after all. They came home from work one day to find a downstairs window in the house next door had been broken. Miss Defreitas's geraniums grew leggy and yellow. The gnome and tortoise were stolen. Olivia kept meaning to ask in the shops if there was any news of their neighbours but as the weeks passed it became too embarrassing to expose her own unneighbourliness in not having visited them. Then one Sunday morning when Nick was buying hot bread for their breakfast the man who served him remarked, 'Shame about old Harry Cartwright.'

'Yes, a great shame. Wonderful old character, old Harry.'

'And her, of course, Miss Whatsername. Pity it wasn't instantaneous really.'

'Yes, it would have saved a great deal of trouble, I suppose – I mean suffering.'

He left with his bread to the pronouncement that something – faulty brakes or drunk drivers – made the shopkeeper's blood boil.

The boards of several rival estate agents were nailed up in the front garden of the house next door. Nick was on the phone to Mark and Annabel at once. They put in a bid, and with a bit of judicious gazumping, their offer was accepted. Olivia and Nick were ecstatic. Summer would be one long spritzer.

Annabel and Mark came over for a celebratory breakfast, a foretaste of the Sundays when they would be neighbours.

'Cheers,' said Mark, raising his glass of Buck's Fizz. 'You'll have to do something about that fence, old man. I believe it's your responsibility.'

A carillon of church bells broke on the summer air like brass confetti, as if in joyful collaboration with the clinking glasses, pealing a benison over the future. At that moment Ruby jumped out of the open window and stalked up the road towards the church, thin and black with her tail at a resolute but pious angle. The cat-flap crashed and Henry strode into the room with something in his jaws. He dropped it in the centre of the circle of friends. Olivia screamed. It was grey and furry and very dead. It could have been a rat or a decaying vegetable. Nobody could bring themself to touch it.

Violets and Strawberries in the Snow

As he lay reflecting on the procession of sad souls who had occupied this bed before him, the door burst open with an accusing crack.

'You know smoking is forbidden in the dormitories!'

'I'm terribly sorry, nurse. I must have misread the notice. I thought it said, "Patients are requested to smoke at all times, and whenever possible to set fire to the bedclothes." '

In the leaking conservatory which adjoined the lounge, puddles marooned the pots of dead Busy Lizzies and the brown fronds of withered Tradescantias, and threatened with flood the big empty doll's house that stood incongruously, and desolate, with dead leaves blown against its open door; a too-easy metaphor for lost childhoods and broken homes and lives. At seven o'clock in the morning in the lounge itself, the new day's cigarette smoke refreshed the smell of last night's butts, whose burnt-out heads clustered in the tall aluminium ashtrays. A cup, uncontrollable by a shaking hand, clattered in a saucer. The Christmas-tree lights were winking red and green and yellow and blue, and on the television, creatures from another sphere were sampling mince pies and sipping sherry in an animated consumer guide to the delights of the worst day of the year. There was port and wine and whiskey and whisky too, and Douglas Macdougal sat among the casualties of alcohol and watched what once would have been his breakfast vanish down the throats of those to whom nature, or something, had granted a mandate or dispensation, those who were paid in money and fame as well as in the satisfaction, which had brought a virtuous glow to their cheeks, that they were imbibing in the national interest. There were no saucer-like erosions under their eyes, no pouchy sacs of unshed tears; and in subways and doorways, on station forecourts and in phoneboxes, in suburban kitchens a thousand bottles clinked in counterpoint. Cheers.

'You were as high as a kite last night when they brought you in.' The man seated on his left pushed a pack of cigarettes towards Douglas.

'Well I've been brought down now. Somebody cut my string. Or the wind dropped.'

A coloured kite crashed to earth; a grotesquely broken bird among the ashtrays and dirty cups, trailing clouds of ignominy.

Although a poster in the hall showed a little girl, her face all bleared with tears and snot, the victim of a parent's drunkenness, it became apparent that not everybody was here for the same reason. A woman with wild, dilated bright eyes glided back and forward across the room, as if on castors, with a strange stateliness, passing and repassing the television screen, and from time to time stopping to ask someone for a cigarette, from which she took one elegant puff before stubbing it out in the ashtray and continuing her somnambulistic progress. No one refused her a cigarette; Douglas had noticed already a kindness towards one another among the patients, and no one objected when she blocked the television screen where peaches bloomed in brandy and white grapes were frosted to alabaster. No one was watching it. The inmates sat, bloated and desiccated, rotten fruit dumped on vinyl chairs, viewing private videos; reruns of the ruins they had made of their lives, soap operas of pain and shame, of the acts which had brought them to be sitting between these walls bedecked with institutional gaiety, or fastforwarding to scenes of Christmases at home without them; waiting for breakfast time, waiting for the shuffling queue for medication.

To his right a woman was crying, comforted by a young male member of staff.

'Just because a person hears voices in her head, it doesn't give anyone the right to stop them being with their kids on Christmas Day.'

'But I'm sure they'll come up to see you, Mary.'

'But I won't be there when they open their presents . . .'

'But they'll come to see you, I'm sure . . .'

Her voice rose to a wail, 'But they don't like coming here!'

The tissue was a dripping ball in her hand. He patted her fist.

'They'll be coming to see you, Mary – it's Christmas.'

Douglas felt like screaming, 'She knows it's fucking Christmas, that's the point, you creep!' but who was he to say anything?

'You don't understand,' she said, and male, childless, half her age, an adolescent spot still nestling in the fair down on his chin, how could he have understood?

Douglas was shaking. He didn't want any breakfast. Although the routine had been explained by two people he hadn't been able to take it in. He was afraid to go into the kitchen where the smell of dishcloths mingled with the steam from huge aluminium kettles simmering on an old gas cooker. He hovered in the doorway for a minute, taking in the plastic tub of cutlery on the draining board, the smeary plastic box of margarine, the cups and plates, inevitably pale green, that belonged to nobody. *Timor mortis conturbat me.* He had been saying that in the ambulance, but mercifully could remember little else. A faint sickly smell clung to his shirt. He had refused to let them undress him, clinging to a spurious shred of vomity dignity that was all he felt he had left, aware of his bloated stomach, and had slept in his clothes. Up and down staircases, down windowless corridors whose perspectives tapered to madness, past toothless old men who mimed at him asking for cigarettes, repassing the women with heavy-duty vacuum cleaners, past the closed but festive occupational therapy unit with a plate of cold and clayey mincepies on its windowsill, past the locked library, he ranged on his aching legs, until at last he found a bathroom. As he washed himself, and the front of his shirt and his stubbly face, avoiding the mirror, the words of a song doubled him up with pain, 'Oh Mandy, will you kiss me and stop me from shaking. . .' He used to sing 'Oh Mandy, will you kiss me and stop me from shaving . . .' when his daughter ran into the bathroom and he picked her up and swung her round and dabbed a blob of foam on her nose. If he had had a razor now he would have drawn it across his aching throat, across the intolerable ache of remembered happiness.

Downstairs again he was given some coloured capsules in a transparent cup, and then it seemed that his time was his own. It was apparent that, a long time ago, a severely disturbed patient had started to paint the walls with shit and the management had been so pleased with the result that they had asked him to finish the job, and then had been reluctant to break up the expanse of ocherous gloss with the distraction of a lopsided still life painted in ocupational therapy and framed in dusty plywood or even one of the sunny postcards which are pinned to most hospital walls, exhorting the reader to smile. The television, with the sound turned down, was showing open-heart surgery; the naked dark red organ fluttered, pulsated and throbbed in its harness of membranes. Douglas turned to the man sitting next to him.

'What do we do now?'

'We could hang ourselves in the tinsel.'

Like several of the residents, he was wearing a grey tracksuit, the colour of the rain, the colour of despair. He held out his hand.

'I'm Peter.'

'Douglas.'

'I was going to walk down to the garage to get some cigarettes, if you feel like a walk.'

Douglas shook his head. His pockets were empty. If he had had any money at the start of this débâcle, he had none now.

'Do you want anything from the shop, then?'

'Just get me a couple of bottles of vodka, a carton of tomato juice, and a hundred Marlboro.'

'No Worcester?'

'Hold the Worcester. A couple of lemons, maybe, and some black pepper.'

'You're on, mate.'

Peter was taking orders for chocolate and cigarettes from the others, then he set out into the sheet of rain. Douglas was summoned to see the doctor, a severe lady in a sari: afterwards he remembered nothing of the interview.

Back in the lounge a ghostly boy watched him with terrified eyes, and gibbered in fear when Douglas attempted a smile; whatever the reason for his being here was, it had been something that life had done to him, and not he to himself; some gross despoliation of innocence had brought him to this state. Douglas watched a nurse crouch beside him for half an hour or more, coaxing him to take one sip of milk from a straw held against his clamped bloodless lips; the milk ran down his white chin and she wiped it with a tissue. This sight of one human being caring for another moved him in part of his mind, but he felt so estranged from them, as if he had been watching on television a herd of elephants circling a sick companion. He might have wept then; he might have wept when Peter returned battered by the rain and dropped a packet of cigarettes in his lap; he might have wept when he held Mary's hand while she cried for her imprisonment and for her children, thinking also of his own, but he couldn't cry.

'Perhaps all my tears were alcohol,' he thought. He picked up a magazine. *Don't let Christmas Drive you Crackers*, he read. *Countdown to Christmas*. He thought about his own countdown to Christmas, which had started in good time some two weeks ago, in the early and savage freeze which had now been washed away by the grey rain.

*

'Slip slidin' away, slip slidin' away . . .' the Paul Simon song was running through his head as he skidded and slid down the icy drives of the big houses where he delivered free newspapers. His route was Nob Hill and the houses were large and set back from the road. 'This is no job for a man' he thought, but it was the only job that this man could find. He had seen women out leafleting, using shopping trolleys to carry their loads, and he had considered getting one himself as the strap of his heavy PVC bag bit into his shoulder, but that would have been the final admission of failure; and the suspicion that nobody wanted the newspapers anyway crystallized his embarrassment to despair.

What struck him most about the houses was the feeling that no life took place behind those windows; standing in front of some of them, he could see right through; it was like looking at an empty film set where no dramas were played out. Beyond the double-glazed and mullioned windows his eye was drawn over the deep immaculate lawn of carpet, the polished frozen lake of dining table with its wintry branched silver foliage of candelabra, past the clumps of Dralon velvet furniture and the chilly porcelain flowers and birds, through the locked french windows to the plumes of pampas grass, the stark prickly sticks of pruned roses in beds of earth like discarded Christmas cake with broken lumps of icing, the bird table thatched and floored with snow and the brown rushes keening round the invisible pond. Latterly, ghostly hands had installed, by night, Christmas trees festooned with electric stars that sparkled as coldly and remotely as the Northern Lights. Douglas conceived the idea that the inhabitants of these houses were as cold and metallic as the heavy cutlery on their tables, as hollow as the waiting glasses.

It was late one morning, on a day that would never pass beyond a twilight of reflected snowlight, that he got his first glimpse of life beyond the glass; there had been tyre marks and sledge marks in the silent drives before, but never a sight of one of the inhabitants in this loop of time. Her hair was metallic, falling like foil, heavy on the thin shoulders of her cashmere sweater; he knew that it was cashmere, just as he knew that the ornate knives and forks that she set on the white tablecloth were pewter. Pewter flatware. He had found the designation for these scrolled and fluted implements in an American magazine filched from one of the cornucopias, or dustbins, concealed at the tradesmen's entrance to one of these houses. He stood and watched her as she folded napkins and cajoled hothouse flowers into an acceptable centrepiece. What was her life, he wondered, that so early in the day she had the time, or perhaps the desperation, to set the table so far in advance of dinner. She looked up, startled like a bird, or like one whose path has been powdered with snow from the feathery skirt of a bird, and Douglas retreated. He retrieved a real newspaper, not one of the local handouts which he delivered, from next door's bin and stood in the wide empty road, glancing at the headlines, with a torn paper garland, consigned to the wind, leaking its dyes into the snow at his feet.

Glasgow – World's Cancer Capital, he read. Nicotine and alcohol had given to his native city this distinction.

'Christ. Thank God I left Glasgow when I did.'

He poured the last drop down his throat and threw the little bottle into the snow, taking a deep drag on the untipped cigarette, which was the only sort which gave him any satisfaction now. He coughed, a heavy painful cough, like squashed mistletoe berries in his lungs, and returned to the room he had rented since he had left his wife, and children. The next time that he saw the woman she was unloading some small boys in peaked prep school caps from a Volvo Estate. She was wearing a hard tweed hat with a narrow brim, a quilted waistcoat and tight riding breeches, like a second skin, so that at a distance it looked as if she wasn't wearing any trousers above her glossy boots. Douglas was tormented by her. He looked for her everywhere, seeing her metallic hair reflected in shop windows, in the unlikely mirrors of pubs which she would never patronize. He stood in the front garden staring at her sideboard which had grown rich with crystallized fruits, dates and figs, a pyramid of nuts and satsumas, some still wrapped in blue and silver paper, Karlsbad plums in a painted box, a bowl of Christmas roses; his feet were crunched painfully in his freezing, wet shoes, his shoulders clenched against the wind; he wanted to crack open the sugary shell of one of those crystallized fruits and taste the syrupy dewdrop at its heart. Once he met her, turning from locking the garage, and handed her the paper. He couldn't speak; his heart was sending electric jolts of pain through his chest and down his arms. He stretched his stubbly muzzle, stippled with black, into what should have been a smile, but which became a leer. She snatched the paper and hurried to the house. If a man hates his room, his possessions, his clothes, his face, his body, whom can he expect not to turn from him in hatred and fear? There was nothing to be done, except to wrap himself in an overcoat of alcohol.

Whisky warmed the snow, melted the crystals of ice in his heart; he skidded, slip slidin' away, home to the dance of the sugar-plum fairy tingling on a glassy glockenspiel of icicles, to find the woman who organized the delivery round of the free newspapers on his doorstep. She was demanding his bag. He perceived that she was wearing acid yellow moonboots of wet acrylic fur. She blocked the door like a Yeti.

'There have been complaints,' she was saying. 'We do have a system of spot-checks, you know, and it transpires that half the houses on your round simply haven't been getting their copies. We rely on advertising, and it simply isn't good enough if the papers aren't getting through to potential customers, not to mention the betrayal of trust on your part. There has also been a more serious allegation, of harassment, but I don't want to go into that now. I had my doubts about taking you on in the first place. I blame myself, I shouldn't have fallen for your sob story . . . so if you'll just give me that bag, please . . . and calling me an abominable snowman is hardly going to make me change my mind . . .'

She hoisted the bag, heavy with undelivered papers, effortlessly on to her shoulders and stomped on furry feet out of his life.

So Pewter Flatware had betrayed him. He turned back from the door and went out to re-proof his overcoat of alcohol, to muffle himself against that knowledge, and the interview with the Yeti on the doorstep, and its implications.

A year ago, when he had had a short stay in hospital for some minor surgery, his voice had been the most vehement in the ward expressing a desire to get out of the place. He remembered standing in his dressing gown at the window of the day room, staring across the asphalt specked with frost, at the smoke from the incinerators and the row of dustbins, and saying, 'What a dump.' The truth was that he had loved it. When he had been told that he could go home, they had to pull the curtains round his bed, but the flowery drapes had not been able to conceal the shameful secret that he sobbed into his pillow. The best part had been at night, after the last hot drinks and medication had been dispensed from the trolley, and the nurse came to adjust the metal headboard and arrange the pillows and make him comfortable for the night. Tucked up by this routine professional tenderness into a memory of hitherto forgotten peace and acceptance, he felt himself grow childishly drowsy, and turned his face into the white pillow and slept. He restrained the impulse to put his thumb in his mouth.

Now he was lying in a bank of snow under the copper beech hedge of the woman with tinfoil hair, a lost dissolute baby, guzzling a bottle. The kind white pillow was soft and pure and accepting; he turned his face into it, into the nurse's white bosom, and slept, deaf to the siren that brought the Silver and Pewter people to their leaded windows at last, and blind to the blue lights spinning over the snow. He was now on the other side of sleep, on a clifftop, wrestling with a huge red demon which towered out of the sea, unconquerable and entirely evil. He woke in the ambulance, gibbering of the fear of death, and was taken to the interrogation room of the mental hospital, in whose lounge he sat now, reading a magazine article on how to prevent Christmas from driving you crackers.

At some stage in the interminable morning, one of the nurses brought into the lounge her own set of Trivial Pursuit, and divided the hungover, the tearful, the deranged, the silent and the illiterate into two teams, but the game never really got off the ground. The red demon of his dream came into Douglas's mind, and at once he realized that it had been the Demon Drink; a diabolical manifestation, a crude and hideous personification of the liquid to which he had lost every battle. But the demon assumed other disguises by day; liquefying into seductive and opalescent and tawny amber temptresses who whispered of happiness, that it would be all right this time, they promised; they would make everything all right and each time that he succumbed he couldn't have enough of them, and their promises were broken like glass, and at night as Douglas lay neither asleep nor awake, the demon took his true shape and led him to glimpses of Hell, or at least to the most grotesque excesses of the human mind. He had not dared to go to sleep in his dormitory bed; all night thin ribbons of excelsior had glittered round the doorframe and the barred windows; it sparkled pink and phosphorescent and crackled in nosegays on the snores of the sleeping men, and danced in haloes of false fire above their restless heads.

'I hate going to bed,' he heard Peter say to a man called Bob, 'it's like stepping into an open grave.' And then, 'I'm so terrified of drinking myself to death that I have to drink to stop myself from thinking about it.' Bob was a big gentle man with broken teeth, and his bare forearms were garlanded with tattooed hearts and flowers. Peter asked him what had happened to his teeth, and about a scar on his hand.

'They sent me up to D ward and the nurses broke my teeth. They broke two of my ribs as well.'

He said it quite without rancour: this is what happens when you are sent up to D ward. Unable to bear the implications of Bob's statement, Douglas concentrated on a somewhat haphazard game of Give Us a Clue that was in progress across the room. Charades had been proposed, and abandoned in favour of this idiosyncratic version of the television game, and

Douglas was invited to join in. As he rose from his chair, he saw that Peter was crying, and he saw Bob reach out his scarred and flowery hand and place it on Peter's knee and say gently through his broken teeth, 'I wish I could help you with your troubles, Peter.'

In his shamed and demoralized state Douglas felt that he had come as near as he ever would to a saint, or even to Jesus Christ. The sight of the big broken man giving a benediction on the other's self-inflicted wounds moved him so that he sat silent and clueless in the game, unable to weep for anyone else, or for his own worthlessness. Then an old man stood up, his trousers hoisted high over his stomach to his sagging breasts. He extended his arm, closed thumb and forefinger together, and undulated his arm.

'What's that then?' he demanded.

'Snake,' said Douglas.

'Yep. Your go.'

Douglas sat; the embodiment of the cliché: he didn't know whether to laugh or to cry.

> 'For When the One Great Scorer comes
> To write against your name,
> He marks – not that you won or lost –
> But how you played the game.'

The debauched Scottish pedant swayed to his feet, grinning uncertainly through stained teeth, and played the game.

In the afternoon his daughters came to visit. He would have done anything to prevent them, if he had known of their intention. He wanted to hide, but they came in, smelling of fresh air and rain, with unseasonal daffodils and chocolates, like children, he thought, in a fairytale, sent by their cruel stepmother up the mountainside to find violets and strawberries in the snow. He took them to the games room which was empty. Here, too, the ashtrays overflowed; those deprived of drink had dedicated themselves to smoking themselves to death instead. The girls had been to his room, and had brought him clean clothes in a carrier bag, and cigarettes. He was so proud of them, and they, who had so much cause to be ashamed of him, made him feel nothing but loved and missed. They laughed and joked, and played a desultory game of table tennis on the dusty table with peeling bats, and mucked about on the exercise bicycle and rowing machine which no one used, and picked out tunes on the scratched and stained and tinselled piano. There was an open book of carols on its music stand: that will be the worst, he thought, when we gather round on Christmas Day to emit whatever sounds come from breaking hearts. Two of the girls lit cigarettes, which made him feel better about the ash-strewn floor, and Mandy, who did not smoke, let no flicker of disapproval cross her face; all in all they acted as if visiting their father in a loony bin was the most normal and pleasurable activity that three young girls could indulge in on a Saturday afternoon. It was only when the youngest said that she was starving, and he said that there were satsumas, which another patient had given him, in his locker, and she made a face and replied 'Satsumas are horrible this year' that they all looked at each other in acknowledgement that her words summed up the whole rotten mess that he had made of Christmas. The fathers have eaten sour grapes, and the children's teeth are set on edge. Douglas broke the silence that afflicted them by saying, 'Good title for a story, eh?' A reminder that in another life he had been a writer. Someone was waiting for the girls in a car, and as he led them to the front door, he hurried them past a little side room where Bob was hunched in a chair, his great head in his hands, his body rocking in grief. Douglas heard the laughter of staff, a world away, behind the door that separates the drunks from the sober. In his carrier bag he found a razor, electric. Now I can shave myself to death, he thought, as opposed to cutting my throat. There were also some envelopes and stamps, a writing pad and pen. There were no letters that he wished to write, but he took the paper and pen, and wrote 'Satsumas Are Horrible This Year', as if by writing it down he could neutralize the pain; turn the disgrace to art. It would not be very good, he knew, but at least it would come from that pulpy, sodden satsuma that was all that remained of his heart.

Later, he went into the kitchen to make a cup of tea for himself and for several of the others: like ten-pence pieces for the phone, and cigarettes, coffee was at a premium here. He was hungry, not having eaten for days, and thought of making a piece of toast, but he did not know if he was allowed to take any bread, and the grill pan bore the greasy impressions of someone else's sausages. He realized then what all prisoners, evil or innocent, learn; that what seems such a little thing, and which he had forfeited, the act of making yourself a piece of toast under your own lopsided grill, is in fact one of life's greatest privileges. He stood in the alien kitchen that smelled of industrial detergent and fat and old washing-up cloths, seeing in memory his children smiling and waving at the door, their resolute backs as they walked to the car concealing their wounds under their coats, forgiving and brave, and carrying his own weak and dissolute genes in their young and beautiful bodies. Violets and strawberries in the snow.

Other People's Bathrobes

HER underwear slipped through his fingers in silky shoals of salmon and grayling; stockings slithered like a catch of rainbow eels. He moved about the bedroom like an assassin, although he was alone in the flat, as if he was watched by eyes other than his own which glanced off the mirror's surface like fish scales reflecting the rainy morning light. Several times when he and Barbara had been together, he had felt that they were not alone; over his shoulder an invisible circle of her friends was whispering, condemning him, warning her. He imagined their nights laid out on lunchtime restaurant tables shrouded in white linen, and dissected with heavy silver knives and forks. He did not know what he was looking for as he went through her things – some evidence as dangerous as a gun lying in the silken nest, that he could possess and use to destroy her when it suited him.

Last night they had come out of the cinema knock-kneed with grief, holding on to each other against the pain of someone else's tragedy. The restaurant smelled of fish and lemon, and clouds of steam banked the lower halves of the windows and evaporated in rivulets down the black glass. He was hungry throughout, and after, the meal. She had eaten almost nothing and her refusal of wine had inhibited his own intake, as the spring water bubbling glumly in its mossy green glass dampened his desire, although her stockinged foot, slipped from its shoe and stroking his leg under the table, suggested that it had refreshed hers.

'I'm sick of mangetout peas,' he had grumbled. 'I want proper peas, without pods, from a tin.'

She had smiled at him indulgently, as at a child, although his petulant mouth was in danger of becoming merely peevish. Meanwhile he salivated discontentedly in memory of the food of his brief happy childhood. A low-slung moon hung in the north London sky as she drove them home; the golden crescent of a pendulum slicing the blackness; it would taste of melon if sucked, a wedge of honeydew. He sat beside her, in silence, aware that he was, as always, in the passenger seat.

There was nothing in the bedroom to incriminate her: dresses gave evidence of nothing that he did not know, shoes were mute and jewellery jangled to no purpose, scent left false trails and no glove pointed the finger. Books that might have betrayed her were not called to witness.

'There are some robes you can use,' she had told him on the first night he had spent with her. That had been three weeks ago and he was still there, still wearing borrowed bathrobes and dressing gowns. This morning he was dressed in a blue kimono with a red and gold dragon writhing up its back and tongues of flame licking his shoulders. He went to the window and lifted the corner of the blind. The trees in the street were hung with leaves the colour of cooked swede, and mashed swede lay in heaps in the gutters; pyracantha flung bright sprays of baked beans against the houses opposite. In his twenty years he had worn too many dressing gowns belonging to other people. He sighed and pulled the sash tighter around his diminishing waist and padded into the kitchen.

He opened the fridge and the freezer compartment and then slammed them shut, sending shivers through the bottles of mineral water shuddering in the door. There wasn't even any real coffee, just that stuff that you had to muck about with filter papers, and a small jar of decaffeinated powder, and a tiny tin of sweeteners instead of sugar. He shook four or five white pellets into a cup and added coffee and a dash of skimmed milk as he waited for the kettle to boil.

'No bleeding bread of course . . .'

He microwaved the lone croissant into a blackened shell and smeared it with low-fat spread. He could have murdered a fried egg sandwich washed down with a mug of hot sweet tea. She, of course, had breakfasted on her usual fare of a tisane and half a dozen vitamin and mineral tablets. He lit a cigarette and took it and the newspaper into the main room of the flat – he never knew what to call it: front room, although it was, or lounge, were wrong – and pushed aside the white vase of black porcelain roses and white plastic tulips and put his feet up. Smoking was frowned on almost to the point of a total ban, but since the early morning when she had sensed his absence in the bed and come into the kitchen and screamed at the sight of his legs sprawled on the kitchen floor, his head wedged firmly in the obsolete cat-flap, a forbidden cigarette clamped in his lips spiralling smoke helplessly into the dawn chorus, she had relaxed slightly the interdiction. She had thought he was dead. It had taken an hour, a lot of soap, and finally a screwdriver to release him.

When he had bathed he would run the Hoover over the carpets; there was little for it to vacuum up except a light frosting of the low-fat crisp crumbs which he had consumed while she got ready for bed. It was the Hoover which had brought them together: he had arrived in response to her inquiry to a cleaning agency and had stayed on to help her prepare for a dinner party, as she moved about the kitchen with a brittle energy that teetered over into panic, her pale hair crackling with electricity in the stormy light pouring through the window. When the first guest arrived it was he who opened the door, a glass of wine in his hand, and entertained them until she emerged from the bathroom where she had fled. She could hardly have arrested in mid-arc the bowl of salted pumpkin seeds he was proffering to her friends and explain that he was the cleaner, and so he had stayed. It was not until they all sat down to eat that she realized that an extra place had been set already at the table.

After the Hoovering he would take her italic list and a plastic carrier bag, as well preserved and neatly folded as if it had been ironed, and wander down to the shops. He took the radio and another cup of coffee and his cigarettes into the bathroom and as he idled in the scented oil watching mingled smoke and steam being sucked through the extractor fan on the window he could not avoid remembering the previous night.

She had wanted both of them to go to bed early because she had had a hard day before they met in the evening, and she was nervous about a sales conference the following morning. The publishing company for which she worked had been taken over recently, and anxiety about losing her job and treachery within the firm had smudged blue shadows under her eyes, and bitten nails, spoiling her gloss, betrayed her fears. By the time Adam had joined her in the bedroom she had fallen asleep; her hair frazzled out like excelsior on the pillow, the tag of a sachet of camomile tea drooping over the rim of the mug on the bedside table. He slid into bed, smelling the sweet-sour odour of the infusion on her breath as he leaned over her face and took her, all flowers and mineral water, in his arms and slowly and cynically began to make love to her. Their hip bones clashed; the morning would see his faint bruises mirrored in milky opals on her skin. He thought that her ambition was to be the thinnest woman in London this side of anorexia, and he remembered reading of a young girl who had almost achieved sainthood by dint of never eating; people had flocked to witness this miracle and marvel at the beautiful and holy maiden pink and white as roses and angel cake, sustained on spiritual food, until one night a nun had been caught sneaking into her room with a basket of goodies. He wondered sometimes if Barbara, too, was a secret snacker but there was never any evidence. He licked the whorls of her ear, as cold as one of her porcelain roses, with the tip of his tongue, while in imagination he piled a plate with processed peas swimming in their bluish liquor, pickled beetroot staining the fluffy edges of a white instant-mashed potato cloud, a crispy cluster of acid yellow piccalilli; he added a daub of ketchup to his garish still life, and then he had to stifle a laugh in her shoulder as she responded because only he knew that the rhythm they moved to was that of a song that had been running through his head since they had got home. Food, glorious food . . . dah da da da dah dah. He had forgotten some of the words he had sung as a ruby-lipped treble taking the lead in *Oliver*; backstage, after the last performance before the last tremulous tear had been flicked from the lashes of the departing audience, Adam had been expelled for extortion. Food, fabulous. Food, beautiful. Food, glor-i-ous food!!! Pease pudding and saveloy, what next is the question? While we're in the mood – Glen Miller took up the baton with a flash of brass and buttons, or Joe Loss, sleek as an otter in a dapper dinner jacket or tuxedo. 'Tuxedo Junction'. And then Adam and Barbara expired together in an ecstasy of cold jelly and custard and he let her drop back on to a steaming heap of hot sausage and mustard. She traced with her finger his lips which were parted in a grin.

'Darling.'

'Best ever?' he asked.

She nodded, smiling and showering the pillow with pease pudding from her hair as he licked the dollop of mustard from her nose.

He had slept badly in an indigestion of shame. Bits of bad dreams lay on his mind, as unappetising as congealing food left overnight on a plate. He watched beneath half-closed lids as she gathered up the clothes she would assume as silken armour against her threatening day, moving quietly so as not to wake him, but each door, each opened and closed drawer hissed her panic. He felt her hover over him for a moment after she had placed a mug of coffee on the coaster on the floor beside him, then with a jangle of keys, a revving of the car, she was gone and he was left floundering in the billows of the duvet trying to sleep away part of the long morning. He wished to spend as little time as possible in the company of someone he disliked as much as himself.

People who had encountered Adam as an angelic-looking child had assumed that he was a good little boy. He shared their estimation of himself until at the age of six years he had been surprised by impulses that were far from good. A girl in his class at the infants' school brought in, one morning, to show the teacher, a dolls' chest of drawers that she had made by glueing four matchboxes together and covering the top, back and sides with glossy red paper, the sort of paper that they made lanterns from at Christmas time. The handles of the drawers were yellow glass beads. Adam coveted and coveted this object all morning. She had allowed him to hold it at dinner play, as long as he didn't open the drawers, and had made him give it back. It was beyond the price of the Matchbox tractor which he had offered in exchange. He could not have said why he wanted the chest of drawers so much: he had no use for it beyond the pleasure of opening and closing the drawers. He could keep matches in it, he had decided, if he had had any . . . perhaps it was because it was so tiny and perfect and because he could not have contrived so neat an artefact with his own clumsy fingers, which behaved in craft lessons like a bunch of flies on flypaper – his Christmas lantern had been a disaster, with the slits cut the wrong way, and had ended up, shamefully, in the waste-paper basket. He brooded through the afternoon story and squinted at it through the steeple of his fingers as they sang, 'Hands together, softly so, little eyes shut tight', plotting. He had hidden behind a hedge after school and jumped out on her from behind, pulling her knitted hat over her eyes, and snatched the chest of drawers and run off. The school was a very short distance from home, with no roads to cross. He was out of sight, although not out of earshot of her wails, by the time she had freed herself from her hat.

'What's this?' His mother was waiting for him at the entrance to the flats.

'I made it at school.'

'Isn't that lovely. Just like something they make on "Blue Peter",' she had said as they went up in the lift.

'It's for you,' he had heard himself say. There was even a pink ring from a cracker in one of the drawers, which fitted her little finger, just above the second joint.

So, eating tinned spaghetti on toast in the afterglow of his mother's kiss that afternoon, he had realized that he could assault and rob and lie; arts which he had polished over the years, after his mother's death when he was ten years old, during his six years in care and throughout his sojourns in squats all over London.

'That's that,' he said to himself as he rewound the Hoover's flex. 'Now for the next item on my thrilling agenda.' As he stowed it away in what she called the 'glory hole', although a neater glory hole than this one with no cobwebs and everything stacked on shelves could not be imagined, his eye fell on a cardboard carton. He pulled it out, not knowing what he expected to find. His heart beat faster as he opened the flaps – a baby's shoe perhaps, a bottle of gin or the heads of her former lovers, as in Bluebeard's Castle, their beards dripping blood. What it contained was books: children's books, schoolgirl annuals, an illustrated *Bible Stories* whose red and blue and gold illuminated sticker stated that it had been presented for regular attendance at St Andrew's Sunday School in a year before Adam had been born, a stamp album with a map of the world on its cover, that released a shower of shiny and brittle stamp hinges like the wings of long-dead insects when Adam set it aside with the thought that it might be worth selling; the books that heap trestle tables at every jumble sale, even to the copy of *The Faraway Tree* by Enid Blyton, with the statutory request in faded and wobbly pencil that if this book should chance to roam, box its ears and send it home, to: Barbara Watson, 59 Oxford Road, Canterbury, Kent, England, Great Britain, the Northern Hemisphere, the World, etc., etc., *ad tedium.* Barbara had been crossed out and Brenda substituted; then Barbara had deleted Brenda, but in vain. The names fought each other in sisterly rivalry all down the page and it was not clear at the end who had triumphed; Adam heard slaps and tears, and the pulling of hair. *Britain's Wonderland of Nature*: a large green volume with a butterfly embossed on its cover and glossy colour plates which must have been her best book, Adam thought. It had been given to her by Uncle Wilf in 1960.

At the bottom of the box was a photograph album. He lifted it out and took it into the black and white room. Perhaps this was what he had been looking for. He lit a cigarette to heighten the experience.

The album had a faded blue cover and crumpled spider's web paper separated the leaves; the small photographs affixed to the storm-grey pages had crimped edges, like crinkle-cut chips, and there, flies in amber and butterflies in glass, was Barbara's past. It seemed that she had spent all her childhood on a beach against an unfailingly grey sky. The photographs were captioned in a loopy adult hand. Here were the infant Barbara and Brenda, the tangled strings of their sun-bonnets blowing towards a sullen sea; a comical snap of Barbara in giant grown-up sunglasses, mouth open in dismay, holding an empty cornet whose unstable scoop of ice cream had evidently just fallen to the beach. Here was Uncle Wilf, with Aunty Dolly at Tankerton – he must have been a widower then, when he purchased *Britain's Wonderland of Nature*, Christmas 1960. Adam pictured him entering the glass doors of W.H. Smith, sleet, like a dandruff of sorrow on the stooping shoulders of his black coat, to buy books for his nieces, the icy wind, or memories of the time he had rolled his trousers and Dolly tucked her skirt up round her knees and stood with the sea gushing between their toes smiling into the camera before she had vanished off the edge of photographs, bringing a tear to his eyes. At Whitstable, Dad, whose name was Ron, Adam discerned, had for some reason come without his trunks and, presumably unable to resist the call of the sea, was wearing what looked suspiciously like his wife's bathing suit rolled to his waist. All the sad south coast resorts were represented in shades of black and white and grey; Adam sat in the room whose colour scheme echoed the childhood tints, his cigarette burning unnoticed in a cube of black onyx striated with white, turning the pages. He had the family sorted out now, grandparents, uncles, aunts and cousins, Mum or Mavis in white shoes, Dad; Brenda and Barbara so close in age as to be almost twins, and no longer bothered to read the captions.

By the age of four or so Brenda had become noticeably plump; beside her Barbara was as frail as an elf. Brenda swelled with the years like a raisin soaked in water; she grew into a quite unfortunate-looking kid. There was one shot of her that arrested him: she stood scowling, with her bare feet planted apart on the shifting pebbles, thighs braced, her solid little body eggcup-shaped, straining the rosettes of her ruched cotton bathing suit, her candy-floss hair parted at the side, and caught in an ungainly bow blowing in the wind that blurred the sails of the toy windmill in her hand, every line of her face and body expressing such defiance and discontent that Adam found himself smiling. Behind her the horses of a merry-go-round galloped in a frieze refrigerated by time. Someone had added a comment in pencil to her mother's writing. Adam took the album to the window the better to see.

'Barbara is a fat pig,' it said, and a pencilled arrow pointed undeniably to the photograph and was corroborated by the words, 'singed Brenda'. It was impossible. 'Barbara is a fat pig, singed Brenda.' So Barbara had been the fat plain one all along. Adam sat down heavily and lit another cigarette. He felt cheated, as if Barbara had deceived him deliberately. Under that designer exterior there was a common little fat girl. It was all a sham. She was no better than he was. He snapped the album shut. Instead of feeling triumphant at finding the weapon he had sought, he felt sad, almost like crying. Then he began to feel angry with Brenda. He flicked through the pages again and noticed that Brenda in each photograph had pushed slightly in front of Barbara, and she was often dressed in organdie and flounces of artificial silk while Barbara was in cotton. Why was Brenda always wearing party dresses to the beach, and an angora bolero, while Barbara was in print with a school cardigan?

'It seems to me, Brenda, that it was you who were the pig. And you couldn't spell,' he said to the Christmas-tree fairy with her bucket and spade. He wondered how many times Barbara had been singed by Brenda. What were Mum and Dad, Mavis and Ron, doing to have such a discrepancy between their daughters? He hoped Uncle Wilf had loved Barbara the best.

He closed the album and put it away in the carton with the other books and closed the cupboard door. He found Barbara's shopping list and shopping bag and set out for the shops. He could not rid himself of the picture of Barbara in the bathing suit with Brenda's cruel caption, and the quotation – he had played Viola in *Twelfth Night* – 'Thus the whirligig of time brings in his revenges', spun round in his mind like the windmill in her hand and the merry-go-round in the distance, and above the jangle of fairground music he heard the teasing voices of Mum and Dad and all the aunts and cousins, and Brenda's taunting laughter. He had been wrong in thinking that Barbara was no better than he was: she was much better. Everything she had she had earned for herself, while he was driven through life in the passenger seats of other people's cars and lounged in other people's bathrobes. More, she had created herself. He stopped dead in his tracks on the pavement, colliding with a woman with matted hair, draped in a shawl of black refuse sacks.

'I'm in love,' he told her.

'Piss off.'

'Yes. Yes I will,' he said and gave her a five pound note from Barbara's purse, which was clawed into her shawl as she spat at his feet. Something amazing had happened. He had fallen in love, for the first time, with a cross little girl holding a windmill at the end of her goosefleshed arm. If she had been singed by Brenda he would erase the burns, like scorch marks from a table. If she wanted revenge he would oblige, on the whole pack of them. If she wanted a white wedding with all the family there, including Brenda whose childhood had been entwined with hers like the strings of two sun-bonnets on a windy day, that was all right with him too. He went into the shop; for him the best part of the movie had always been when the guy arrived at the girl's apartment with a paper sack of groceries with a fifth of bourbon sticking its neck out: to him that was New York: romance. Unbeknownst to herself, Barbara bought herself a bottle of champagne. As he walked home with his love feast in a plastic carrier bag he saw that the pavement was strewn with litchi shells, broken to show their sunset pink interiors, like shells on a beach in the rain. Outlined against the hectic light everything assumed a poignancy; a bag of refuse and a broken branch of blue eucalyptus made a haiku on the wet kerb. He felt healed, as if someone had poured a precious jar of alabaster over him.

He was in the kitchen when he heard her key in the lock. She stepped inside, all unawares, in her black raincoat rolling with ersatz pearls, coming home to a steaming bowl of Heinz vegetable soup, just like mother used to make.

The Thirty-first of October

IT was the time of year when people stole down garden paths to lay huge woody marrows and boxes of wormy windfalls, and jars of sloppy chutney with stained paper mobcaps on each other's doorsteps, but not on hers. There would be no sparklers on November the Fifth either, although, not five hundred yards away the young men and boys of the village had been building for weeks an enormous bonfire, a superstructure of wood, branches, mattresses, tyres and junk and garden refuse, on the village green; now it was almost complete; a sign ordered that there should be brought NO MORE RUBISH, and members of the bonfire committee were taking turns to sleep out in a little wooden shelter in its shadow to guard it from premature pyromaniacs. A spit had been erected and stood in readiness for the pig that was to be roasted; the early morning air of that day would be tainted with the smell of oozing tissues until a bruised cloud of cooked meat drizzled droplets of fat into the evening air, which would linger for days while the bonfire smouldered, mingling with the grey ash that would coat her front garden and invade the house through the ill-fitting windows. Once she had joined in the procession, but now the prospect of the burning torches of pitch, the faces in the lurid light, the Guy dragged on a rail filled her with dread, evoking other primitive rituals, witch hunts and sacrificial blood spilled on the fields. She leaned against the window, staring into the darkening afternoon, waiting for absolutely nothing at all.

After an Indian summer, the first frost had wrecked the gardens, leaving the hydrangeas in blackened ruins that hulked on either side of the gate that led on to a rutted lane. On the other side of the lane stretched fields. The house next door, one of a pair of cottages, had double-glazed aluminium-framed picture windows, and a snouty little porch of bottle glass, and sliding patio doors at the back. A slice of varnished oak beside the front door bore the name Trevenidor. When she and Paul had moved in he had fantasized that the house had been named in sentimental tribute to a Cornish resort where their neighbours had honeymooned, but when they met Trevor and Enid it became apparent that they had intertwined their own names in a true-lover's knot. Trevor and Enid had two daughters, Kimberley and Carly; now seven and five years old.

She had been pleased by the fact that there were children next door; she had thought that they might alleviate the loss of her own two daughters who were both living abroad, but she blushed now to recollect her fantasies of little figures draped in floury aprons, their pudgy fingers dimpling as they pressed the raisin buttons into gingerbread men, their faces rosy in the warmth of her spicy kitchen; of collecting wild flowers and blackberries and nuts with two little yellow-haired companions. There *were* hazelnuts, and blackberries in the hedges, but they were small and bitter and splashed with grey mud and sprayed with pesticides; and once a year Trevor drove down the lane with a mechanical ripper that tore the tops off the bushes, leaving the branches stripped bare; broken and bleeding. In the first flush of neighbourliness she had offered to baby-sit, but she had been rebuffed. On Enid's darts night Trevor stayed at home, and on the rare occasions that they went out together, Enid's mother, an even larger version of her daughter, was ensconced in Trevenidor. Carly and Kimberley had met her overtures of friendship with silent, bright blue-eyed scorn, clinging to their mother in a parody of shyness, burying their faces her short skirt, pulling it round her columnar thighs until they were slapped off like mosquitoes, and when their new neighbour had extended a biscuit to her, Carly had burst into tears, as if it had been a stone or a serpent; and then later she had heard her name tossed mockingly over the hedge – 'Claw-dee-ya, Claw-dee-ya.'

In the winter frost formed patterns on the insides of Claudia's windows and snow drifted in, dredging the sills like icing sugar. Last year she had steeled herself to confront Trevor over the hedge and ask him to look at the central heating; the bottom halves of the radiators remained cold, while the tops gave out such feeble heat that she could see the clouds of her breath. Trevor, risking Enid's displeasure, for she had referred pointedly to him as My Husband ever since Paul's departure, squatting on his haunches, exposing more of his lower back than Claudia would have wished to see, gave the radiator a shake, causing a tiny avalanche of plaster behind the damp wallpaper and pronounced, 'Not much I can do. I know the cowboy who installed it – your whole system's corroded.'

'I'll just have to turn it up, then . . .'

'You can turn it up as high as you like, lady; you'll always be cold.'

His words left her with the chill of the grave.

She went to the dining table which she used as a desk, picked up a book, and let it drop. It was one that she should have been reviewing, but the deadline was slipping away. 'What was your book called again, only I couldn't see it in the van?' Enid had asked early in their acquaintance. Claudia had not explained that the mobile library was unlikely to carry two books that had been out of print for years, and thereafter she had avoided the van lest she encounter Enid in its crowded interior. She had been highly praised as a miniaturist once, and in vain did she remind herself of little bits of ivory; her talent had diminished until it had disappeared. She depressed a key of the disused piano; damp felt struck rusty wire, and the note hung in the air. A silvery blight was stealing over the veneer, clouding the flowers that wreathed the candleholders. It was Paul's piano, and Enid had asked him not to play it in the evenings because it disturbed the children.

Soon Kimberley and Carly would be home from school, and when darkness had fallen they would come pushing and giggling up her path, pinching each other's arms in their simulated terror, for all the world as if they were Hansel and Gretel, and she was the wicked witch. Trick or treat. What could possibly be a treat to them? The hedges and ditch testified to the chocolate bars and lollies they consumed daily on the way home from school, and although it was only late October they had anticipated Christmas already by devouring the contents of two mesh stockings, filled with sweets, one of which had blown into Claudia's garden. As she had shaken a slug from its interstices and put the torn stocking in her dustbin, she had felt a pang of pity for the children for whom there was no magic. What they would like most from her was money. She had seen their money boxes; pink ceramic pigs with lipsticked snouts and flirtatious painted eyelashes and grotesque rumps, bearing little resemblance to the inmates of the asbestos and corrugated iron stalag whose stench drifted across the fields when the wind was in the wrong direction, where Trevor worked.

Two weeks previously, by a blunder on the part of a secretary, Claudia had been sent an invitation to a party given by her erstwhile publisher. Turning it over and over in her hands, she had searched it for a sign that it was a practical joke, but there was no one who would think her worth playing a joke on. Except Kimberley and Carly, who, last Hallowe'en, had emptied her dustbin on her doorstep; it hadn't been funny but she had heard Enid and Trevor laughing. She had stood the invitation on the mantelpiece, beside the jar of shrivelled rosehips, for all, that is herself, to see. She had taken the bus to the town, where she had found at last, in despair, a diaphanous dress in the Help the Aged shop, but it had been so cold on the night of the party that she had had to wear her kingfisher blue chunky cardigan, bought from Enid's catalogue in more halcyon days, bulkily uncomfortable and protruding its cuffs from the sleeves of her coat.

In the confusion of her arrival in the loud room, where the heat, after her cold walk from the tube, had turned her face to fire, she had forgotten to deposit her cardigan with her coat. Finding herself ignored and jammed up against the drinks table, there had been nothing to do but help herself to red wine. Once, she turned and met the shock of her face; eyes bloodshot with drink and smoke, and a red clownish patch on each cheek, brilliant under the electrified chandelier, above the wrongly buttoned cardy; but by then she had been too far gone to care. She had realized at once that she would have done better to have come in her jeans, as others had, to have pretended a casualness that she hadn't felt; her attempt at finery was so far from the chic of those women who had dressed up. For them, she supposed, this was just another evening, somewhere to stop off before going out to dinner, or home, but she, shamefully, had invested all her hopes in it, and they died among the cigarette butts and broken pretzels and rejected gherkins on the table behind her. When, as she was burrowing for her coat, a woman spoke to her, and, recognizing her name, said that she admired her work, Claudia had been so grateful that she had latched on to her, and found herself one of a party billowing down the road to a restaurant. She was happy; she was back where she ought to be; she felt a sudden conviction that her talent, after all, had not deserted her.

Only the next morning, sitting on the first train home, travelling with a gang of railway workers, apart in a corner, the picture of debauchery in her laddered tights, aware of their gentle mockery, had she realized that she had not been invited to the restaurant. Her pinched cold face flooded with blood as snatches of the evening floated among the black specks in front of her eyes; she had babbled of the pig farm and conjured up Enid and Trevor and Kimberley and Carly to sit among the guests partaking of whitebait and avocado, plonking bluish knuckles and bloodied, half-severed trotters on their plates. Now she felt as alienated from her fellow-diners as she did from her neighbours, and from the men with their sandwiches and newspapers, their camaraderie, their sense of being in the right place at the right time. It was then that she looked down and saw the tidemark of mud on her shoes, that must have been there all the time, adding the finishing touch to her garish rig; and putting her head in her hands, discovered that somewhere in the debris of the evening, lost perhaps on her gallop to the station for the last, missed, train, lay an earring, one of her only valuable pair, given to her by her grandmother.

The irrecoverable loss of the earring burned in an opalescent pain in her throat, as if she had swallowed it, long after the inflammation of the self-inflicted social wounds had abated. The earrings had been promised to her daughter, and at some time the loss must be discovered, or confessed. The end of the evening was a merciful blur, and she would never see those people again, but the earring bereaved of its twin would be an everlasting token of her disgrace.

Her anger at herself turned on Trevor and Enid. She had moved her bedroom to avoid the grunts that she imagined came through the wall, but she lay sleepless in her cold bed, in the musty smell of mildew whose spores she sometimes thought pervaded her own skin, warming herself with a scenario in which Trevor had somehow mistaken his wife for a sow, and Enid lay helpless on the slatted floor, unable to speak or to turn, squeezed between the metal sides of the farrowing pen, subjected to the torments that he inflicted unthinkingly daily on his charges; and then Trevor himself, pale, bristly boar, was driven with sticks up the ramp of his own lorry, squealing with fear, en route for the abattoir.

Changing her room to escape the pork and crackling of Enid

and Trevor's intimacies meant that she was woken by the dawn chorus from Kimberley and Carly, each of whom seemed to rise each morning with a renewed ambition to earn her sister a smack; she had to put her pillow over her head to blot out the sounds of their play which came through so clearly that Claudia, sick with insomnia, almost felt the hair yanked out of her own head and teeth puncturing her own skin. They had plastic kitchens and castles and typewriters and sewing machines and cassette players, vanity sets galore; Sindy dolls and Barbie dolls and Cabbage Patch dolls and Care Bears, Rainbow Brites, Emus, and My Little Ponies complete with grooming parlours for their silky pink and turquoise manes and tails; but the girl's real favourites were two life-sized baby dolls who shared a twin buggy. These two babies vied with each other in naughtiness, but being the progeny of such mothers, they weren't very good at it and their mischief was uninventive and repetitive; nevertheless, it was always severely punished. Had they had any sense they would have unbuckled themselves from their buggy and legged it over the fields in their Babygros to the NSPCC, but being mercifully senseless, they smiled their vinyl smiles and took whatever was coming to them; unlike Tiny Tears, who wept throughout the proceedings and refused to be toilet trained despite the penalties incurred.

But one day the children's grandmother had brought them someone whose arrival left all the other toys in a neglected heap. Orville was an apricot poodle puppy, with overflowing eyes that left the tracks of tears down the sides of his face, giving the impression that he was always crying, which was perhaps a true one. Kimberley and Carly were beside themselves; here was a real live baby who did spectacularly rude and naughty things. He was squeezed and cuddled and was expected to obey their every command and whipped with his little lead until even Enid protested; he was yanked by the neck until he whimpered for mercy; and plastic earrings were clipped to his ears and ribbons tied to his tail. When he had soiled Enid and Trevor's duvet, Claudia could only applaud silently his magnificent *coup de théâtre*, but she could not tell if it had been by intention, or simply because his stomach had been squashed too hard; and of course the consequences for him had been dire.

Claudia had thought that Orville was an uncharacteristically inventive name, until she had discovered that he had been called after an ingratiating, lime-green, fluffy duckling, a ventriloquist's dummy with a plastic beak, who wore a nappy; she had seen the puppy Orville in a makeshift nappy one day, strapped into the buggy, with one of the naughty twins' bonnets on his head; when she had remonstrated with the children, Enid had shouted at her through the open window to leave the kids alone. A few days later she had met them coming home from school.

'Where's Orville?' she said.

'He had to go to the vet's because he chewed up the wallpaper,' replied Carly.

'Will he be all right?' she had asked, stupidly, and then she had realised that she had quite misunderstood.

'And it cost £5.99 a roll,' said Kimberley.

'Come on you two!' shouted their mother, seeing them fraternizing. 'You'll miss your programme!'

'We're getting two gerbils instead,' Carly shot back over her green quilted shoulder as they ran off heavily, in their white latticed knee socks.

'God help them, in their cage . . .' Claudia thought.

'I don't think that's a very good idea,' she called after them.

'None of your business, you old ratbag,' came faintly down the lane.

Old ratbag. Old. Ratbag. Their words hurt far more than they should have; after all, they were only children. She reminded herself that she had always got on with children. She hurried on; the thought of her own children made her feel as desolate as a scarecrow, with the freezing wind whipping the rags of her self-esteem. They had taken her name and made it ugly – Claw-dee-ya, Claw-dee-ya; they had made her ugly. What was a ratbag? She knew what it meant, but what was it?

She could go and knock on their door and say, 'Sorry to bother you, Enid, but could you tell me what a ratbag is? Perhaps you could look it up in your *Pears' Cyclopedia*?' Slam.

She was trapped as surely as the gerbils in their cage. There was no work available locally and she could not afford to move. Next month she must default on the mortgage. Buying a house in the country had been, she saw now, one of the death throes of a desperate marriage. When Paul had left, by mutual consent, and the first heady inflorescence of being alone had evaporated like cow-parsley in July, she had found the freedom to gaze uninterrupted for hours over the flat fields of rape, inhaling the odours of the pig farm; she had fields of time, acres of time, stretching as far as the eye could see, to an uncertain horizon.

A headache zigzagged at her temple like a little firecracker as she stood at the window. She had no aspirin to alleviate it, and could not borrow any from Enid, who anyway was out, collecting the girls. Each morning, after walking them to school, Enid heaved her hams on to the minibus which transported workers to the pharmaceutical research laboratories, where she was employed in the canteen, serving lunches to the animal technicians, and one of the perks of the job was that she never ran short of painkillers and cold cures and vitamin drinks.

That Hallowe'en morning Claudia had walked to the village to pick up the magazine that she had ordered. Foolishly, she had told the woman in the shop the reason that she wanted it. The woman had already checked it out. The story wasn't there.

'I was wondering if you wrote under another name . . . ?' she said.

'No. No I don't.'

The fiction editor in her glitzy office, of course, could neither have known or cared that, miles away, beyond the rim of her consciousness, stood a small woman in wellingtons in a sub-post office in her public shame, concealing under an Army surplus jacket something that resembled a breaking heart.

'Hope deferred. Hope deferred. Hope deferred maketh the heart sick,' her boots beat out on the rutted lane; her fingers numb round the rolled-up magazine, the glossy cylinder that contained someone else's story. The lost earring came into her mind.

'Swings and roundabouts,' she said to herself as she passed the deserted recreation ground. It was absurd to care so much, but that story, in a magazine too prestigious to be among the shop's regular stock, had been going to vindicate her, to prove to Enid, and thence to everybody, that Claudia had some status in the outside world, and to earn her, if not friendship, at least some grudging respect; and also to reassure herself that she still existed. Next month's would be the Christmas issue, and it was unlikely that her muted autumnal tale would take its place among the glossy gift-wraps, the shimmering scarlets and greens and golds of a feast that she would not be celebrating.

It was almost dark, and as Claudia pulled the curtains for the night, at four o'clock, Kimberley and Carly passed her window, their yellow silky hair streaming under black pointed paper witches' hats, their pointed noses, red from the cold air, pecking towards each other in conspiracy, wagging their hats towards her house and laughing, before they ran indoors.

Claudia went into the kitchen and took her sharpest knife and sharpened it. As she worked, she expanded her fantasy to include Kimberley and Carly, naked, trussed and basted, glistening with fat, their crispy skin criss-crossed and stuck with cloves, oranges stuffed in their mouths. She was very hungry; she had not eaten all day. When she had finished her preparations, she sat down in the dark to wait for the children.

They were a long time coming. She sat on the edge of her chair, straining her ears for their steps, hearing only a car door slam, down the lane, the dull explosion of a far-off firework, the blood beating in her head. She put a log on the fire and lit the candles. Everything was ready; so why didn't they come?

The table floated on the darkness like an altar and on its surface glittered a long knife.

The gate moaned on its hinge. There was the sound of footsteps, a shuffling on the doorstep; then the knock. Claudia flung open the door, with a low triumphant cry of 'Trick!'

The hiss died on her lips. There was a confusion of a woman's face above a paper sack from which protruded the neck of a bottle of wine and the white jagged heads of chrysanthemums. It was the woman from the party.

'Oh dear, I can see you weren't expecting me. Have I got the wrong day? That would be typical of me – I thought you said – I brought these . . .'

'Come in.'

Claudia held back the door, and her visitor stepped in, still prattling in her nervousness, into the flickering light and smell of melting wax. 'I do apologise – I was sure – I'll just put these down – I left the car down the lane . . . oh, a real fire, how lovely. And a turnip lantern!'

'Oh that –' said Claudia, glancing at the wicked face, lit from within by a guttering candle, 'it was just a little surprise for the children . . . Here they are now. Would you give it to them?'

Her shadow swooped over the ceiling as she picked up the lantern and held it out to her *dea ex machina*, with nails that gleamed in its light like blood.

'I'll just get rid of this.'

She carried the knife into the kitchen and dumped it in a pile of peelings in the sink.

All the Pubs in Soho

THE pansies were in a blue glazed bowl on the kitchen table, purple and yellow, blue and copper velvety kitten's faces freaked with black, and also in a bed by the back door where they straggled on leggy stems round the drain and the leaking water butt. There was not a trace of blood. Joe's father's words had conjured up a wreckage of broken flowers streaked and spattered with red; the scene of a gory murder. An innocent bee investigated the absence of a crime.

Joe could not understand why they had provoked his father to such rage at breakfast making him choke on bitter marmalade, spitting a jellified gout of rind on to the newspaper. It had reminded Joe of the time a girl with a bad cold had sneezed on to her sum book, and Miss Hunt had ripped out the page and carried it at arm's length to the waste-paper basket, and he had felt sick at breakfast as he had then, when he had also burned with sympathetic shame. Beside the blue bowl of pansies a bluebottle grazed in spilled sugar and negotiated a white papery onion, which was actually garlic, but Joe, like most of the population of Filston, Kent in 1956 was unacquainted with this pungent bulb. A bunch of brushes stubbled with paint stood in a jar; there was a smell of turpentine and paint and linseed oil, the nicest smell that Joe had ever known.

That summer the Sharps, that is Joe, his two little brothers and their parents Peter and Wendy, he of the camel-hair coat and thin moustache and crimped waves of rusting hair, she of the Peter Pan collars and velvet hairbands, had moved into their tall white house set back from the main village street behind a black railing hung with rest-harrow, and had furnished it with blows and tears and cold cocoa and unemptied potties.

Not long afterwards two strangers had descended from the London train and had been observed taking turns to haul a heavy suitcase along the High Street and up the hill towards Old Hollow Cottage. They wore American plaid shirts and jeans, which men did not wear in Filston unless they were of the bib-and-brace working overall variety. The small dark one had slung over his shoulder a dark green corduroy jacket and the taller fair one carried a jacket of muted claret. They were reported to have been drunk on arrival, but this may have been apocryphal information, supplied by hindsight. It was a long walk, uphill on the narrow road between dry banks bulbous with the grotesque roots of the overhanging trees while clouds of midges nibbled the heavy air and sweat ran into their eyes, as far as the crossroads where a broken signpost rusted in a little island of grass and ox-eye daisies, then downhill between fields of cows in pasture and ripening corn to the hollow that gave the cottage its name. That night they cruised into the car park of the Duke's Head with a shrieking of dry brakes, on an old black bicycle they had found chained with cobwebs among the nettles in the shed; one working the brakes and the other perilously side-saddle on the crossbar. Their hands were stippled with nettle sings. They had not had to do anything more scandalous to become notorious.

It was his father's vituperation about 'those bloody pansies at Old Hollow' that had brought Joe to the cottage on this empty summer holiday afternoon. He had had nothing else to do.

Under the table, on the wine-coloured jacket, a wild-looking black and white cat, with burrs and green knobs of goose grass in her fur, was stretched out, nuzzled by a heap of squeaking multicoloured kittens. Joe stepped over the threshold and crept towards them.

In the bedroom at the back of the one-storeyed cottage the fair-haired young man lay on his side on the bed smoking, reading and from time to time looking at the dark one who was sitting in a creaking wicker chair, wearing only a pair of jeans, drawing him; sunshine leaked round the sides of the yellow curtain pulled crookedly across the window, brushing his skin with bloom, turning his hips into a peach, blue smoke from the cigarette in his trailing hand swirling in the lemony light. There was a faint mushroomy odour of mildew in the room. Suddenly a tenderly drooping line became a gash in the paper as the artist dropped his pencil and ran from the room.

'What –?'

The fair man felt too lazy to follow. He returned with a struggling figure clasped to him, its legs kicking at his shins. Its T-shirt, stained with elderberry juice, was pulled askew, scratched legs kicked from the khaki shorts.

'Look what I found in the kitchen.' He let go with one hand and flung a pair of jeans at the bed.

'Cover yourself up.'

The fair man pulled the bedspread cover over himself. The child was struggling and snarling in the captive arms.

'Good afternoon,' said the man on the bed as he struggled into his jeans. 'Who are you?'

The child was trying to bite now, making futile lunges with its teeth, snapping the air.

'I think it's a wild boy of the woods,' said the fair man. 'Abandoned as a baby and brought up by the wolves.'

'There aren't any wolves in England,' snarled the wild boy with distinctly middle-class scorn.

'What excuse have you, then, for breaking and entering? Have you come to spy on us? Or to steal?'

'I only came to see the bloody pansies!'

The dark man released him. He stood panting and rubbing his arms where they had been held. The two men looked at each other, then the fair one said in a silly voice, 'Well, here we are, duckie. Allow us to introduce ourselves. I'm Arthur and this is my friend Guido.'

The child gave an uncertain giggle, looking from one to the other.

'Don't be silly.'

He was beginning to think that they might not murder him, even the fierce dark one, Guido.

'I knew we shouldn't have come here,' said Arthur.

'Who are you then?' Guido asked the child.

'Joe.'

Arthur raised himself on an elbow and studied him.

'Are you sure it isn't Josephine?'

A blush ran down Joe's freckled face and neck and out of his sleeves and down his arms.

'If he says it's Joe, it's Joe,' said Guido sharply.

'Well Joe, what do you say to a cup of tea?'

Joe nodded, too mortified to speak. There was the air of a stray dog following the stranger who patted his head in the street about him as he followed Guido into the kitchen without looking at Arthur.

'How old are you, Joe?'

'Nearly nine.'

Guido filled the kettle and put it on the stove. The smell of gas mingled with the turps and linseed oil filled Joe's head, and mixed with his excitement at being there and having tea with two grown-ups was the odd feeling that he was completely at home.

'Are you an artist?'

'A painter. Do you like painting?'

'Well – I can draw an elephant from the back, and a star without taking the pencil off the paper. Shall I show you?'

'That's OK. I believe you. Can you carry the tray into the garden? I'll go and get Arthur.'

Joe carried the round tin tray carefully and set it in the grass.

He lay on his back and watched the sky. The sound of raised voices came from the kitchen. Joe sat up at once, tensed to run. He felt sick. The child from a house where a veneer of anxiety lay on every surface like dust, where at any moment a bark might rip up comics and scatter toys, where a fist thumping the table might make cups leap in fear vomiting their contents on to the tablecloth, just as Joe had once been sick when his father caught the side of his head with his knuckles, and where Mummy's forehead wrinkled like the skin on cocoa and her chin puckered in fear and placation, expected every domestic disclosure between two adults to degenerate into a battle in which by being co-opted to one side, he was considered the enemy by the other, and so always ended as the loser whoever else was in power when a truce was called. But then Guido and Arthur came out together to join him. Arthur was holding a whisky bottle.

'I thought we'd have a wee celebration, as Joe's our first visitor.' He poured whisky into two cups.

'To Joe.'

'Joe.'

Gradually Joe stopped shaking enough not to slop the strong red tea from the cup which Arthur handed to him: it was the most beautiful cup he had ever seen, a pearly white shell that stood on tiny china periwinkles on a flat fluted saucer – Beleek, a legacy from Arthur's Irish grandmother.

He realized that no one would have told him off if he had slopped it. The cake was dry and crumbled like sand on a plate painted with a blue fish. They were sitting under an old apple tree hung with small red apples. Joe looked up into its branches and then at Guido, for permission.

'They're very sweet,' said Guido.

Joe reached up and an apple fell into his hand. The skin was warm and the white flesh did taste sweet. They sprawled in the grass and talked; Guido and Arthur smoked, Joe ate apples and cake. They accepted what he said without once telling him not to be silly, or to stop showing off or not to interrupt or not to dip his cake in his tea and scoop out the residue of crumbs and sugar with his finger. It all went to his head like whisky. Suddenly something in the light told him it was late. He sat up abruptly, his old panicky self. 'I've got to go. I've just remembered someone's coming to tea. I'll be late. What shall I do?'

'Take the bike,' suggested Arthur.

'But –'

'You can bring it back tomorrow.'

Joe, swooping and curvetting down the hill, straddling the crossbar, standing on the pedals, clenching the screaming brakes, the heavy black handlebars bucking in his hands, heard over and over again the words, 'You can bring it back tomorrow,' and made them into a tuneless song that was snatched by the wind whistling past his ears.

He came into the room on the awful words from his mother's visitor.

'So it's to be St Faith's then?'

She disposed of Joe with sponge cake in her mandibles.

'No!' he shouted. 'I won't.'

The glory of the afternoon fell from him as he confronted the wavering tableau of his mother's shocked face above a new pale blue necklace, the best teapot garlanded with roses floating in her hand above the tablecloth, his brothers' smeared faces above the trays of their high-chairs, the yellow and red wedges of cake.

'Josephine, where on earth have you been? I specially asked you not to be late for tea. I don't know what Mrs Williams will think of your hands and face, and put on a clean frock at once.'

'I'm not going to St Faith's.'

As Joe backed from the doorway, it was what Mrs Williams would think that was uppermost in his mother's mind: that she was a poor mother who could not control her plain and disobedient daughter, that the little boys were noisy and not toilet trained, that the blue outlines of the transfer still showed at the edges of the satin-stitched flowers on the tablecloth that she had just finished embroidering that morning and had not had time to wash or iron, and that already a stain was seeping though the linen on to the table beneath the cloth. A bad mother and a bad housekeeper.

'Well, it seems the best of a rather poor bunch,' she whined, referring to St Faith's as if her disparagement of the local educational establishments might attach some credit to her disappointing daughter.

Joe was not a pretty child. Now her freckles stood out on her blanched skin against the red and white gingham dress that was quite wrong for her colouring, as her mother and Mrs Williams realized simultaneously. 'You might have brushed your hair,' her mother despaired. 'She insists on having it short although it doesn't suit her,' she apologized, regretting the ringlets that might have been.

'Nice and cool for the summer, eh?'

Mrs Williams gave a conspiratorial pat to the sweaty reddish feathers glued to the mutinous forehead. Joe tossed her hand away.

'I'm not going to St Faith's, I'm going to the village school and I'm not going to wear a stupid hat, and I'm not . . .'

'Just drink your milk. She likes to play at being a boy, I'm afraid . . . I can't think why.'

'I don't.'

'Please don't keep interrupting. The grown-ups are talking. Help yourself to bread and butter.'

'I've had tea. With my friends.'

Wendy sighed and turned away.

'Another cup of tea, Mrs Williams? Oh dear, I'm afraid the pot's gone cold.'

Joe sat silent, a milk moustache framing her savage mouth, her stomach turning to scrambled egg at the thought of walking through the village in the uniform of St Faith's. Even if she crumpled the hat and hid it in her satchel, there could be no concealment. It was hopeless. If she could do something heroic, rescue one of the other children from the river or a fire, maybe they would forget the way Daddy had shouted at them and chased them from the garden. If only she could wake up tomorrow morning and be a boy and have a suit of grey shorts and a jacket with a zip and elasticated waist and cuffs – Roy Noble had a dark blue corduroy suit, that was the best, but she would settle for a threadbare grey, worn with gumboots – and he had a television. She had heard his mother call, 'Roy, it's telly time,' and he had run in leaving her alone in the rec holding on to Timothy's pushchair.

'. . . Nancy boys . . .'

The words clattered on to her empty plate.

Mrs Williams went on, '. . . so she went up to him in the shop and said, "Mr Morelli, I'm the President of our local Artists' Circle, and I wondered if you'd like to come for coffee one morning and meet some of our members", and do you know what he replied?'

'No. What?'

Mrs Williams leaned towards her and lowered her voice.

'He said, "You know what you can do with your blankety-blank coffee"!'

'No!' Wendy gasped.

'Can you imagine? In Carter's!'

'My husband says that people like that ought to be shot. I mean to say, it makes my flesh crawl, just to think – ugh.' She shuddered, holding out an arm so that they might see the pale hairs express their horror.

'There are men who love other men, just as there are women who love other women,' said Joe.

'Leave the table at once!'

'There's nothing wrong with it. Just because someone loves somebody they get put in prison and people call them all –'

'That's enough! I don't know what's got into you this afternoon.'

An unmistakable smell that could not be ignored was staining the disastrous tea party.

'Josephine, take Timmy to the bathroom and wipe his hands and face, and bring him back and then go to your room.'

Her eyes signalled desperately that Joe should change Timothy's nappy, as if there were a chance that Mrs Williams had not noticed.

'What can a little girl like you know about such things?' Mrs Williams's voice held reproach for the whole family.

'I just know.'

'I can't think where she – neither Peter nor I would dream of discussing such matters in front of a child . . .'

Joe did just know, she thought, as she yanked Timothy from his chair. When Guido and Arthur had talked to her, it was as if she had always known, but had just been waiting for someone to say it. She had known too, without being told, that she should say nothing of her visit at home.

'Love between men. Love between women,' Wendy thought, as with increasing embarrassment she realized that she had told Josephine to remove the wrong child. Away from the magazines she read, in the real world inhabited by Peter and herself, in the marital bed lumpy as semolina, there wasn't even much love between men and women.

'Would you like to look at the garden?' she asked, and called, 'Oh, Joe, look after Giles, would you?'

A big old black bicycle, a heap of junk, was sprawling on the lawn.

Carter's, where Guido had ground the Artist's Circle under his heel like a cardboard disc whose triangles graduate through the shades of the spectrum, was the biggest shop in the village. There was Dawson's, which was handy for sweets, for a packet of fags on a Sunday, and a branch of the South Suburban Co-operative Society, but people like Wendy did not shop there. Carter's had a wooden floor that sloped down to the glass-fronted biscuit containers that fronted the mahogany counter, a wire for cutting cheese, a red bacon slicer, bins of dried fruit and glass jars of sweets, and a wines and spirits licence. The back of the shop smelled of paraffin and Witch firelighters and neat bundles of chopped firewood bound with wire and aluminium buckets and coal scuttles and clothes pegs and new rope. Fruit and vegetables were displayed at the side entrance. The emporium was owned by Mr Carter, who presided over the bacon and cheese and cold meats and wines and spirits, and was staffed by seven part-time assistants known collectively as the Carter girls. Each was mysterious in her own way, but it was Dulcie, the youngest, who conceived a passion for Arthur.

Dulcie had been engaged, and her fiancé, called up for National Service, had been killed. Her future was hacked to pieces on the mud floor of a hut in Kenya. Her fiancé's dismembered remains lay under a white marble gravestone in Filston churchyard and her dreams were split by savage painted faces and flashing knives. She had been cheated of her rights, and had had to sell her ring back to the shop at a loss to help to pay for his funeral, and had been condemned to remain with her miserly widowed father on a squalid smallholding called Phoenix Farm. It became a joke among the other Carter girls that Dulcie blushed when Arthur came into the shop. Her usually bitter mouth simpered, her offhand manner became solicitous as she packed his shopping bag.

'Mind them eggs,' she would say as she placed them carefully on top of his purchase, or, 'You ought to take somethink for that cough.' Other customers could arrive home with dripping bags of a dozen broken eggs, or cough themselves to death for all she cared, but she worried about Arthur. She picked her way past the steaming heaps of sodden straw through the mud in her high heels, carrying over her arm an overall washed every night and starched as white as chalk in the hope that he might come in. She was disappointed if Guido was with him but it was better than nothing. Shc could not understand why Mr Carter was so against them and she thought it slightly peculiar that neither of them was married, but that was her good luck. Mr Carter had installed a new refrigerator, and stocked its shelves with new exciting ice creams. As usual, when they entered the shop, fine ice crystals of disapproval frosted the air round Guido and Arthur as they hovered at the throbbing fridge, unable to agree which flavour would most please Joe.

'The Nealopitan's very nice,' suggested Dulcie, her face burning in the chill.

'Eat Nealopitan and die,' said the funny foreign one.

'No, honestly, it's ever so nice,' insisted Dulcie, offended. Anyway it would have melted by the time they got it home.

On the afternoon of her half-day Dulcie was slouched at the bus stop contemplating the prospect of plodding round the shops of the nearest town, then catching the bus home again to get her father's tea. Boredom twittered in the hedges, crawled among the flints of the wall on which she leant and grazed the green slope of the opposite hill. She threw her half-smoked cigarette into the road, just for something to do. She was twenty; she should have been coming up to her second wedding anniversary in a new house on the new estate. It wasn't fair.

Incredibly, she saw Arthur walking down the empty road towards her. She prayed that the bus would not come.

'Fancy meeting you here!' she stuck out her thin hip and put her head on one side. It did not seem a very surprising or unlikely meeting to Arthur.

'Hello.'

He didn't alter his pace.

'Coming to the dance?' she called after him. He stopped.

'What dance?'

'That one. A week Saturday.' She pointed to a poster that announced a Grand Dance, to be held in the Village Hall.

'I don't dance.'

'Oh go on, it's a good laugh. I'm going,' she added as an incentive.

Arthur hesitated, not knowing what to say, watching a string of black and white cows crossing the hill, beyond the brittle rainbows of the split ends of her hair. He had quarrelled with Guido and stalked out of the house, propelled by his anger until stopped by this girl.

'What's your name?' she was saying.

'Arthur.'

'Arthur.' She sounded disappointed. 'That's nice. You're not foreign are you, like your friend?'

'Scottish.'

'Oh. Your friend though, he's foreign, isn't he?'

'An Eye-tie. A wop. Second generation.'

'I thought he was foreign. Aren't you going to ask what my name is then?'

'No,' said Arthur, exhausted by this interchange.

'Oh, you are awful,' she slapped familiarly at him. 'It's Dulcie. Silly isn't it? I hate it.' She heard with alarm the rumble of the bus round the corner. 'You coming to the dance, then?'

'I told you, I can't dance.'

'I'll teach you. Go on, it's a laugh. Eight o'clock Saturday, I'll see you there,' she called over her shoulder as she swung on to the bus, and then she slumped into a seat exhausted by her own daring. By the time the bus had reached the town she was convinced that not only had she and Arthur a firm date for Saturday week, but that *he* had asked *her* to the dance. She bought a pair of shoes and matching handbag, and a bag of sweets which she popped rapidly and mechanically into her mouth, crunching without tasting so that when she got off the homeward bus she was surprised to find an empty bag in her hand. She stood for a moment in the field stroking the shiny patent leather of the shoes and handbag before going upstairs to hide them from her father under the floorboard, with her mother's empty blue shell of Evening in Paris, and her bottle of California Poppy.

Meanwhile Arthur had sat on a swing in the deserted rec behind the Village Hall where the Grand Dance was to be held, smoking and scuffing his feet in the dusty trough worn by the generations of children's feet. When the packet was empty and he had tossed it over his shoulder, he suddenly laughed and left the swing performing a wild parabola on its rusty chains, and was whistling when he dropped into Carter's for more cigarettes. If, like Dulcie, Mr Carter thought that Arthur looked like a movie star, it was of no film that he would care to see; his manner was within a moustache breadth of offensive as he handed over a bottle of bad red wine and rang up the inflated price on the till. Arthur, for his part, gave not a thought to the absent Dulcie, who might have served him. He wished that he had the bike so that he could get home faster. Guido was lying asleep on the bed, open mouthed, smelling faintly and sweetly of stale white wine.

He was always Joe at the cottage. Once Guido had got on the bus and had seen him and Wendy sitting there in Mother and Daughter polka-dot frocks, made by Wendy from a Simplicity pattern, which had proved not so simple, and Joe's polka-dot hairband had slipped round to show the elastic. He never knew if Guido had seen them or not and neither of them had referred afterwards to the encounter. Wendy would have been surprised to discover that she had become a smoker; her account at Carter's showed evidence of cigarettes and of chocolate and other delicacies which she had not consumed. Carter's was so handy, she just gave Josephine the list and she did most of the shopping. Arthur and Guido were doubtful when Joe gave them presents and hesitant about accepting them, but he was so hurt if they refused that they took the gifts.

'You don't have to bring us presents, Joe. We enjoy your company. Just bring yourself.' Joe did, as often as he could. The kittens were growing adventurous and Poppy, the mother, was quite friendly now, her coat almost glossy; Arthur had found her in a field with her neck in a snare and had brought her home and nursed her and she had rewarded him with a litter of kittens two days later. Joe played with them or talked to Guido while he painted, receiving grunts in reply, or bashed about on Arthur's typewriter or gathered mushrooms which they fried in butter until they were black. Nobody told him not to touch the matches, or not to lick his knife or not to pick the blisters of hot paint from the back door. The corn in the field next to the house was almost ready to be cut, the blackberries in the garden were flushed with red, the heavy red tomatoes splitting their sides and breaking their stems. Guido had cleared a patch and had planted squash and zucchini, and they fried their yellow flowers, fluted like the horn of the gramophone that poured music on to the garden, in batter. In the front room there was a broken sofa and piles of books which had come from London in a van with Guido's easel. Joe looked at the pictures, turning over the thick and glossy pages heavy with damp in the mushroomy air and read poetry which excited him even though he did not understand it; he loved the feel of the foreign books printed on thick paper with rough edges, he felt that if he could read them they would tell him everything that he wanted to know, although he did not know yet what that was. At home at night he lay in bed listening to the rise and fall of voices below, his body tensed for the modulation that was the signal for him to put his pillow over his head.

One afternoon, having escaped at last from amusing Timothy and Giles, Joe was so startled to hear a loud woman's voice over the hedge that he swerved violently on the bike, bruising himself agonizingly on the crossbar. He rolled in silent screams on the grass, buffeted by the woman's laughter and alien men's voices. He stood outraged on the edge of the gardens pierced with jealousy. Several other men and Arthur and Guido were lounging about in the grass and, on a kitchen chair, like a queen among her courtiers, was a black-haired woman. The worst thing, the thing so shocking to the child who flicked unperturbed through books of painted nudes, was that she had taken off her blouse and sat in her brassière. Joe stared in horror as a kitten crawled between those shocking white circle-stitched cones. His freckles fused in a dull red stain, but the woman was not embarrassed, and neither, it seemed, were any of the men. He had never seen Mummy in anything less than her petticoat, four thin straps slipping down her sloping shoulders as she brushed her hair, and this lady was much older than Mummy.

'Come away, Joe, and have a drink.' Arthur's voice was more Scottish than usual. 'This is Joe, everybody, the wee friend we was telling you about.'

Joe came forward, avoiding looking at the woman, but she grabbed his arm and pulled him towards him. She thrust her face into his with a clacking of earrings.

'Guido, where did you find this enchanting little redhead?'

She ruffled his hair. He wriggled away. The kitten leapt from her chest, puncturing a breast with a hind claw. She screamed. A tiny bead of blood rolled on to the white brassière.

'I'm bleeding, Arthur, do something –'

'It's only a little scratch,' said Joe, his voice thick with scorn. He picked up the kitten and stroked it, comforting it.

'Anyone would think that it was that creature who was wounded, not me. Doesn't anybody care that I'm bleeding to death?'

'Oh shut up, Cathleen, and have another drink.'

She squeezed the last drop of blood from the tiny wound. Arthur splashed wine into her glass. Incredibly to Joe, he did not seem to hate or despise her. Joe turned to Guido but he was talking to a horrible man with a stained moustache that curled wetly into the corners of his mouth. Joe could not believe that Arthur and Guido liked these people, but they were laughing and joking with them as if they had really missed them.

'Whatsa matter, Joe?' called Arthur, and gulped as an unripe blackberry thrown by Cathleen landed in his mouth.

'Nothing,' said Joe.

Everybody looked ugly. Arthur's eyes were bloodshot, his lips too red. 'He looks like a wolf,' thought Joe. Pieces of wolves' dinner, chicken bones webbed with sticky skin lay in the grass, rejected by the kittens, the air was heavy with smoke and wasps attacked the carcass of a cream cake. A squashed wasp lay on the open book beside Cathleen's chair. They were all talking loudly about people Joe had never heard of. He went into the kitchen. Guido followed him.

'Look at this mess!' said Joe in his mother's voice, waving an arm at the table piled with greasy plates and smeared cutlery and glasses and crusts and dirty paper napkins. The lovely smell of paint and linseed oil was glazed with stale cooking.

'Poor Poppy, you hate them too, don't you?' said Joe picking up the cat who was cowering under the table and receiving a scratch from a flashing paw, which he scorned to notice.

'Why so sulky, Joe? Come into the garden and amuse us. Tell us all the gossip.'

'Don't know any,' said Joe.

Wendy, had she been otherwise, would have found a rich source of gossip in Mrs Cheeseman who came in to clean two mornings a week, but her nervousness manifested itself in a shrill bossiness, and Joe could see that Mrs Cheeseman despised them. She was the widowed mother of two teenage daughters, Ruby and Garnet, and had four cleaning jobs as well as keeping her own house immaculate and winning most of the prizes at the Horticultural Show. Her stoicism on her widow's pension put the Sharps to shame. Joe had once seen her throw a piece of his Meccano from the bedroom window.

'Don't be jealous, Joe. It's very dull for Arthur here with only me to talk to.'

'And me.'

'And you too, of course.'

'And the cats.'

'And the pussy cats.'

Joe went back outside to hide the tears in his eyes just as Cathleen pulled Arthur on to her lap, pressing him against the squashy white cones and nuzzling his ear.

'Aw, get off, Cathleen, will you.'

'Not until you give me a kiss.'

Arthur pecked at her cheek.

'Not like that. A proper kiss. What are you staring at?' She turned on Joe who stepped back from the savagery of her eyes.

'Nothing.'

'Like hell you are. I do believe it's jealous. Arthur, has our little freckled friend got a crush on you by any chance?'

'Leave him alone Cathleen.'

Guido had come out into the garden, his face snouty and mean with alcohol. It wasn't clear whom he meant Cathleen to leave alone.

'Such a waste,' Cathleen said to Arthur. 'You're much too pretty.'

'I said, lay off. Arthur, you look like a clown, but you're not funny.'

Cathleen had smeared a red cupid's bow on his forehead, and another on his cheek.

'What's wrong, Guido? You're not jealous too, are you? Of me, a mere woman? Stop being such a tedious old queen. Here, Freckles, stop gawping and get me another drink.'

She thrust out her clownish tumbler.

'Don't stick your fingers in the glass. Where are your manners?'

'I was trying to rescue a fly,' said the erstwhile enchanting little redhead.

'Oh for God's sake.'

Arthur had struggled free but she kept hold of his hand. He squatted beside the leg of her chair, whose feet were embedded in the grass by her weight, with her rings digging into his hand. He did not look unhappy. The man with the stained moustache began to sing; the petals of the last rose of summer blew about on a beery wind while tears ran down his cheeks.

'Guido. Guido.' Joe pulled at his arm. Guido shook him off.

'Look, why don't you go and pick some mushrooms?'

'I did.'

Joe flung the paper bag of mushrooms to the grass and burst into tears. Everything was spoiled. He blundered towards the bicycle to escape from the party of badly behaved adults. Home seemed almost a haven. Then he felt an arm round him and he was pulled to Arthur's chest.

'What's all this about? Hey, come on . . .'

He took a handkerchief and dabbed ineffectually at Joe's eyes and tweaked his nose until he had to laugh.

'That's better. Come away into the kitchen and have a cup of tea with me.'

'You still look like a clown,' said Joe.

'Well, at least I made *you* laugh.'

When they returned to the party everybody was in a good

mood. Guido said that it was his birthday next week and that he and Arthur were coming up to London to celebrate and that everybody must join them.

'We'll bring Joe,' he said. 'We'll take him to all the pubs in Soho.'

'Look at his face,' said Cathleen. 'Look at that wicked grin. Such decadence in one so young,' but she said it nicely. And she had put on her blouse. Joe forgave her. He was prepared to love her. He accepted a sip from her glass and then another and let himself be pulled on to her knee. The gramophone poured Euridice, Euridice in its scratched voice over the garden.

The trees reared up crazily at him as he zigzagged down the hill, a little drunk. 'All the pubs in Soho. All the pubs in Soho,' sang in his ears. Soho shone over the horizon, a golden city of shimmering spires where he would go with Guido and Arthur and be happy.

'I picked you some mushrooms.'

Joe stood in the doorway of the bathroom holding out the crushed paper bag which he had retrieved from the grass and forgotten to leave in the cottage kitchen.

'They're probably toadstools. Put them in the bin at once and wash your hands.'

'No, they're definitely mushrooms. We've had them lots of times.'

'Who's had them?' she asked sharply.

'Me and my friends.'

She hauled Giles out of the bath.

'You haven't been playing with those rough children again, have you? You know what Daddy said. I don't know what he'd say if he knew you'd been picking toadstools. It's absolutely forbidden, do you understand?'

She stared in exasperation at her unnatural child in the stained khaki shorts, her lips stained with what must be blackberry juice, clutching a bag of poisonous fungi, and turned to Giles who was lying across her lap. Despite her ministrations his bottom was sprinkled with the sore stars of nappy rash.

'Mummy?'

'Yes.'

'What's Soho?'

'It's a place in London. A not very nice place.'

'Why not?'

'Well – pass me the baby powder please.'

'Why not very nice?'

'Will you keep still, Giles. Timothy, if you get off that pot once more, Mummy's going to be very cross.' The baby squirmed in her lap.

'Why isn't it very nice?'

'Because not very nice people go there. Now will you stop asking silly questions and make sure Timothy stays on his pottie? It's not the sort of place people like us go to.'

'Hah,' said Joe.

It was obvious that Mummy knew nothing about Soho. He saw its name in letters of gold shining through the powder and steam. It was exactly the sort of place people like himself went to.

The floor of the village hall was dusted with talc for the feet of the dancers and dusty silver twigs were stuck into green-painted tree stumps for decoration. Crates of beer, and more ladylike drinks, were carried across from the pub and stacked on the trestle-table that formed the makeshift licensed bar and coloured light bulbs looped the stage where the band stood; the bare bulbs that hung from the ceiling were dressed in crêpe paper skirts, and bunches of balloons attracted ribald remarks. The Grand Dance, after a sticky start, was in full swing. Dulcie danced with the first man who asked her, Geoff Taylor, who had always fancied her, although she did not fancy him, tossing her head vivaciously, studiously not looking at the back of the hall where the summer night streamed through the double doors, so that Arthur might arrive and see her in another man's arms, dancing with the lights sparkling in her hair. She had not seen him alone since their meeting by the bus stop and had interpreted his every word as secret confirmation of their date and had read all sorts of romantic implications into his most mundane request. She pictured him lounging in a dark suit and white shirt with a red carnation in his buttonhole, a cigarette between his lips, watching her. She was a good dancer but her new shoes hurt. After four or five dances with different partners she stood by the bar sipping orangeade through a straw watching a wrinkled balloon deflate. The band played on. Incipient blisters throbbed on her heels. She giggled hectically with a group of girls, then danced again, desperate that he should not arrive to find her wilting like a wallflower; her smile was fixed in fresh lipstick on her face, her eyes were now unable to keep off the door. Only the knowledge that she had told no one that Arthur was coming to the dance – she had been saving that triumph – saved her from bursting into tears but in the penultimate dance, the Carter girls hokey-cokeying wildly, her face dissolved and she rushed from the hall, tearing off her shoes and running blindly barefoot across the recreation ground.

Feet pounded after her and Geoff Taylor caught her arm, swinging her round to face him as the last waltz smooched out among the stars. She sobbed against his chest the story of how Arthur had asked her to the dance and stood her up.

'Him? That queer bloke?'

She nodded, not understanding the adjective.

'I'll bloody kill him.'

She blew her nose, too miserable to be ladylike.

'I've got the bike. Do you want a lift home?'

Soon she was on the back of the motorbike, her arms clasped round his waist, holding her shoes with the heels sticking into his stomach as they blasted up the village street, towards Phoenix Farm, her skirt billowing out behind her like a parachute.

As Arthur passed the Duke's Head on his way to the post

office he was seduced by the smell of warm beer in the sunshine through the open cellar door. The landlord slopped down his pint on the counter with no more than the usual contempt. A tractor stopped and a young man jumped down and followed him into the bar which was empty except for two old men in caps playing dominoes and a dog-faced woman in tweeds morosely sucking a Mackeson while a little dog died quietly at her feet. Pipe smoke was caught in the golden cones fluting through the bottle glass and turned them blue. In the morning air the polished glasses and horse-brasses among the low beams had the clarity of a hangover; a strong smell of hops came from the dusty dry garlands on the ceiling and from the clear brown beer in Arthur's glass. He felt a frothy head of well-being wash over his boredom. He looked at the young man who had followed him, taking in the faint and not unpleasant scent of old manure around the patched dungarees, the brown arms under the rolled sleeves of the faded workshirt, the scowling face under a cowslick of Brylcreem. Incongruously, he was drinking whisky. Arthur raised his own glass and nodded to him but the young man obviously drowning his sorrows at 11.30 on a summer morning spat a flake of tobacco from his lip and shoved his empty glass across the bar for another shot.

'Going it a bit, aren't you Geoff?'

One of the old men called out. Geoff uttered something incomprehensible to Arthur and they all laughed, one of them choking wetly on his pipe stem, and Arthur found himself smiling too. He ordered another beer; he had no desire to leave this pleasant place. The onslaught of the second drink prompted him to conviviality. He almost ordered drinks all round, but he had only enough money left for stamps. In his inside pocket was an envelope containing poems which he was posting to a magazine in London.

Reluctantly he went out into a morning gold and blurred at the edges, the road ran like a river at his feet. Suddenly he was on his back on the asphalt with grit and blood in his hair and Geoff Taylor's fist smashing into his mouth and an iron-capped boot chipping at his legs while its owner exhorted him to stand up and fight. He tried to get up grasping handfuls of road and was kicked back with a boot in the chest. His head caught the kerb. Bone bounced off stone. A wild blow glanced off Taylor's stomach and Arthur grabbed his shirt and pulled himself up and and landed a punch on his jaw which sent him reeling back on his feet and followed it through but missed as Taylor stepped aside. Arthur's head was a broken ball of pain; he could taste blood in his mouth. He tried to grab Taylor round the waist to throw him but his legs buckled and he collapsed on his knees. Taylor's fist crunched again into his face and withdrew bloody, then he kicked him systematically all over his body and finally stamped on his outstretched hand.

The tractor's engine sputtered away into silence. Arthur could hear a blackbird singing in the watery tones that herald rain. His whole body was in pain. He knew that his hand lay, an injured creature, in the road beside him. 'It's a good thing it wasn't Guido. I can write with my left hand,' he thought, then red and black swirled, dissolved as he lost consciousness.

The president of the local Artist's Circle saw him lying in the gutter, and crossed the road. It was only what she would have expected of him.

Clinging on to hedges and walls Arthur managed to stagger as far as Carter's where he leaned on the door and fell into the shop with a jangling of its bell.

'Help me.'

'Get out of my shop,' said Mr Carter who was cutting cheese with a wire. The Carter girls in their white overalls stood like monoliths behind the counter. Dulcie gave a little scream and started forward.

'Get back to your work, Dulcie.'

Dulcie looked at the bloody misshapen bruised swede that had been her idol trying to speak through lips glued to its teeth with blood.

'Yes, Mr Carter,' she said and started weighing broken biscuits.

'We don't want your sort here,' said Mr Carter. 'Get out, and mind my clean floor. Go back where you came from.'

Arthur crawled out. He made it across the road to the surgery and swayed in the little porch hung with Virginia creeper leaning on the bell. The doctor's wife answered.

'Yes?' she asked.

'Doctor.'

'The doctor's having his lunch. I suppose you'd better come into the surgery and wait.'

She left him slumped on a fumed oak chair whose chintz cushion was tied on with tapes. He had to brace himself to stop from sliding to the floor.

'You have got yourself in a mess, haven't you?' she said as she closed the door behind her.

Eventually the doctor came, clouded in evidence that he had enjoyed a small cigar after his lunch.

'This is going to hurt,' he said with satisfaction, expecting Arthur to wince and mince, and Arthur screamed silently with the effort not to play the role expected of him as the doctor swabbed and strapped his ribs with distaste.

'You ought to have that hand X-rayed. And your head,' he concluded without telling Arthur how to go about it. 'You'll live,' he said.

Arthur tried to thank him.

'Don't thank me. You're not one of my patients, thank God, so I'll be sending you my bill. Know where you live, but what do you call yourself?'

Arthur looked at the red cloudy water in the basin and sodden lumps of cotton wool like obscene red snowballs, and fainted.

'Pull yourself together, man. How are you going to get home? Can you pay for a car if I get you one?'

Arthur nodded. He just wanted to be with Guido. He didn't know if Guido would be able to pay but he was past caring.

The local taxi service was operated by the landlord of the Duke's Head, and so it was he who dumped Arthur on the cottage doorstep and stood jiggling coins in his blazer pocket while Guido ran to find the money for his exorbitant fare.

'You should have seen his face,' he told his customers in the bar that evening, 'when he saw the state of little Miss Nancy. I though he was going to burst into tears.'

Wendy, who was there with Peter, almost felt sorry for Guido for a minute, but the thought of two men kissing made her feel sick: she could not conceive that they might do anything but that.

'Perverts,' said Peter.

'If there weren't ladies present . . .' said the landlord.

Two ginger cats, named Gin and Lime, one smooth, one fluffy, smirked on the bar. Wendy didn't really like leaving the children alone in the house but Peter got so cross if she made a fuss, and Joe was quite capable . . .

'You're looking very pretty tonight,' said Peter. 'That sherry's brought quite a sparkle to your eyes.

'Thank you kind sir,' she said, with dread.

All the cats, Poppy and her kittens, ran at Joe when he pushed open the kitchen door.

'Guido? Arthur?'

He went into the garden. They weren't there. His heart started to race; a sick feeling came into his stomach. The silence had a quality of finality, as if the air had closed for ever on the spaces left by bodies, and voices were gone without echoes. He ran back into the kitchen ignoring the importunate cats. There were two notes on the table. One was addressed to the woman from whom they had rented the cottage, and one to him.

Dearest Joe,

I expect you've heard what happened. We are going back to London and then to the south of France where Cathleen has a house.

Please look after the pussy cats.

Will write. In haste,

Guido. Arthur.

Arthur's name was shaky, as if written with his left hand.

'No,' cried Joe, 'you can't, you can't,' in desperate belated entreaty. He ran out into the road and gazed at its achingly empty blue curve, the edges fretted with birds' songs and skirmishes. 'Come back! I want to come with you. What about me?' he shouted. 'What about all the pubs in Soho?' He sank sobbing onto the grass verge. 'Come back! Come back!'

A rough furry head thrust into his wet face purring loudly.

He opened a tin of pilchards and while the cats ate he read again Guido's note. What had happened? He had no idea. Why couldn't they have taken him with them? Wild thoughts of burning the letter to the landlady and living in the cottage himself rushed through his brain and were swamped by reality the colour of cold cocoa. Guido and Arthur were the only bright colour and affection he had known and they were gone leaving him entirely alone. The thought of St Faith's inspired more tears.

He went into the bedroom. A torn and stained shirt had been thrown into a corner. Joe picked it up, screamed, and dropped it. It was stiff with dried blood. He thought Arthur had been shot.

'Please don't be dead. Please don't be dead. Please don't be shot.'

But Arthur had signed the letter so he couldn't be dead.

Joe took the shirt and lay on the bed with it in his arms rocking from side to side as he wept.

From time to time a sob still shuddered in his chest as he gathered up Poppy and the kittens and struggled to get them all into a large cardboard box which he tied round and round with string. It took him almost an hour: as soon as he had pushed down one wild head or paw another sprang out. At last he carried the squeaking wailing box outside and left it by the bicycle at the front hedge. He went into the field and dragged a bale of straw through the hedge and into the kitchen. He took the bottles of turpentine and linseed oil and methylated spirit from the draining board and splashed them over the straw and round the kitchen, and went into the bedroom. Tacked to the wall was a little sketch of Arthur lying on the bed. He tore it out and put it in his pocket, and splashed methylated spirit over the bed. He took a box of matches from the kitchen table and set fire to a corner of the sheet and to the corner of the bale of straw.

The journey home wheeling the bike with the cats bumping awkwardly on the saddle was agonizing. His back hurt with the effort of balancing the box and although he had draped it with the bloody shirt he had to stop every few steps to push back a terrified head. He knew that if one got out he would never get it back again. The spinning pedal hit him sharply on the ankle many times until his leg was a mess of oil and blood. The chain came off and dragged rustily in the road. His grief was overtaken by his dread of what would happen when he got them home.

He came into the kitchen. Daddy was home early.

'Look what's come for you. Isn't that a lovely surprise? It came from Peter Jones this afternoon,' said Mummy. There was an enormous box on the table. It must be a present from Guido and Arthur. His heart leapt.

'Well open it then,' said Daddy impatiently.

Joe lifted the lid and parted the tissue paper. Inside lay the brown velour hat with a yellow striped band and the brown serge wrap-around skirt and yellow blouses of St Faith's School.

'Well, you might at least try to look pleased,' said Daddy. 'This little lot cost me a small fortune. What on earth have you been doing? Your face is disgustingly filthy. Let's hope St Faith's will –'

Mummy, who had been twisting nervously at her blue poppet beads, broke them and they went pop pop pop over the kitchen floor.

'I only hope you realize how lucky you are.' Daddy's voice went on.

But at that moment Joe realized like a blow to the stomach that Guido could not write. He didn't know the address. He picked up the hat and threw it on the floor and stamped on it. His father's hand caught him across his tear-stained face. Joe seized the hand and bit it.

'I hate you, Daddy, you tedious old queen,' he screamed, kicking his father in the shins.

Behind him in Old Hollow, the cottage blazed like the fires of hell; the cats burst out of their box in the shed, and the nude study of Arthur fell to the floor in his rage.

Where the Carpet Ends

THE Blair Atholl Hotel was berthed like a great decaying liner on the coast at Eastbourne; if it had flown a standard from one of its stained turrets it would have been some raffish flag of convenience hoisted by its absentee owner, flapping the disreputable colours of the Republic of Malpractice and Illegality.

The front windows had a view of the Carpet Gardens and the pier, but the back of the hotel, where Miss Agnew lived, gave on to the drain pipes and portholes of another hotel and a row of dustbins where seagulls and starlings squabbled over the kitchen refuse. Miss Agnew, impelled by the vicissitudes of life to book a cabin on this voyage to nowhere, was one of the off-season tenants who occupied a room at a reduced rate at the top of the hotel, where the carpet had ended. These people of reduced circumstances were required to vacate their rooms just before Easter when the season started, or pay the inflated price required of summer holiday-makers. After the third floor, the mismatched red and black and orange carpets gave way to cracked linoleum and, in places, bare boards. A terrifying lift, a sealed cage behind a temperamental iron zigzag door, carried them up to their lodgings, separated from each other by false plywood walls that divided what had once been one room into two compartments. One floor above them, huddled precariously like gulls, perched a colony of homeless families, placed there by the council in bed and breakfast accommodation, whose misery filled the pockets of the landlord and his manager.

If, as Le Corbusier had said, a house was a machine for living in, the Blair Atholl, thought Miss Agnew, was a machine for dying in; but at least there, unlike the residents of the many old people's rest homes in the town, they were doing it on their own terms. The residents of the fourth floor formed a little community in exile, rescuing each other when the lift stuck, knocking on a door if someone had not been seen about, purchasing small sliced loaves for the sick and Cup-A-Soup and tins of beans to be heated on the lukewarm electric rings, and braving doctors' receptionists, in the smelly telephone booth, to beg for a home visit but dreading above all an admission to hospital, from which one so seldom returned. They met in the conservatory at the back of the hotel in the evenings for a rubber of bridge or to watch a programme on the television, which was a reject from the lounge, whose horizontal hold had gone, and formed a little human bulwark against the sound of the sea and the approaching night. It did not do to think too much, Miss Agnew had decided; to dwell on people and cats and dogs and houses in the past was to inspire one to board the next bus to Beachy Head, but sometimes she could not resist stopping to speak to a cat or a dog in the street, and the hard furry head and soft ears under her hand evoked lost happiness so painfully that she strode away berating herself for laying herself open to such pangs, her red mackintosh flapping like the wings of a scarlet ibis startled into flight.

She did not know why antagonism had flared up between herself and the manager, Mr Metalious. She paid the rent on time and she was surely no more bizarre than any of her fellow residents: the Crosbie twins, seventy-year-old identical schoolboys who dressed on alternate days in beige and blue pullovers they knitted themselves, and grey flannel trousers and blazers. She felt sure they would have affected caps with badges if they had dared; they did wear khaki shorts in the summer and long socks firmly gartered under their wrinkled knees. Or than the transvestite known as the Albanian, a smooth-haired shoe salesman who by night flitted from the hotel, a gauzy exotic moth, to sip the secret nectar of the Eastbourne night. Or than Miss Fitzgerald who left a trail of mothballs and worse in her wake and cruised the litterbins of the town and rifled the black plastic sacks her fellow tenants left outside their doors on dustbin day. Or than Mr Johnson and Mr Macfarlane who spent their days philosophizing in the station buffet. Or than the Colonel whose patriotism embraced British sherry. Or than silent Mr Cable. Or Mrs MacConochie. Miss Agnew thought that perhaps she reminded Mr Metalious of some teacher who had humiliated him in front of the class, or a librarian who had berated him for defacing a book. She had followed both these professions in her time, but she was not interested very much in his psyche, and anyway videos were more in his line than books. Perhaps she had alienated him when, on moving into the hotel, she had asked him to carry her box of books to her room. He had acquiesced with a very bad grace, telling her that his duties did not include those of a hall porter: perhaps her decision that he would have been offended by a tip had been the wrong one. Whatever the cause, and even before she had overheard him refer to her as a stuck-up old cow, she knew he did not like her.

'Nothing today, Miss Agnew,' he would call out as she passed her empty pigeon-hole beside his desk.

'I wasn't expecting anything,' she told him truthfully, but he was determined to regard the lack of post as a confirmation of her low status and as a triumph for himself.

Anyone less bovine than Miss Agnew would have been hard to imagine; she was more ovine, as befitted her name which she believed to derive from the French, with her long mournful face framed by a fleece of off-white curls. Now that it didn't matter any more, she was thinner than she had ever hoped to be. The most she had hoped for in this town, which she had more than once heard referred to as 'God's Waiting Room', was anonymity. She was desirous to be known only as Miss Agnew and she expected nothing more of her pigeon-hole than dust or a catalogue for thermal underwear, and why he picked on her for this particular humiliation she did not know. None of the residents got much post, except the Albanian who received thin cobwebbed envelopes addressed in a spidery hand, and the Crosbie twins who corresponded copiously with each other in the course of each of their infrequent quarrels.

It was lunchtime and Miss Agnew was seated at a table in the window of Betty Boop's, a small vegetarian restaurant that suited her herbivorous taste, ruminating over a piece of leek flan. She had managed, by taking very small mouthfuls and laying down her knife and fork between each bite, to prolong her meal for twenty minutes or so, when she saw Miss Fitzgerald pass, head bowed against the wind to avoid a spume of salty vinegar being blown back into her face by the north-easter from what was undoubtedly someone else's discarded bag of chips.

Since a recent survey had condemned Eastbourne as a town of guzzlers, Miss Agnew had become aware of the habit of the populace of snacking out of paper bags; the precinct was sugary with half-eaten doughnuts, meaty with burgers and strewn with the polystyrene shells that had held pizza and baked potatoes, the toddlers under the transparent hoods of their striped buggies clutched buns and crisps and tubes of sweets; and now there went Miss Fitzgerald conforming, for once, to a local custom.

Miss Agnew was thinking about Beachy Head; it was comforting to know that it was there. When she had walked there in the summer she had been dazzled by the colour of the sea, opal and sapphire as in Hardy's poem 'Beeny Cliff', and she had felt a melancholy empathy for the writer because for her, as for him, 'the woman was elsewhere . . .' and nor knew nor cared for Beeny or Beachy Head and would go there nevermore. Miss Agnew had felt a powerful force pulling her to the cliff's edge, and only the thought that she would probably plummet messily on to the boiling rocks rather than curve like a shining bird through the sky into the iridescent sea had propelled her backwards on the turf. The Crosbie twins had told her that many more bodies were recovered than were reported; the local police and press had a policy of suppressing such information, *pour décourager les autres*. She wondered how largely Beachy Head loomed in the minds of her fellow residents.

Now she gulped down her elderberry wine, paid the bill, and succumbed to an impulse to follow Miss Fitzgerald, feeling amused at herself and more than slightly ridiculous as she turned up the collar of her mac like that of the trench coat of one of the private eyes in the detective stories she used as a drug against insomnia when she lay awake in the night and felt the hotel slip from its stone moorings and nose towards oblivion. She tracked her quarry past the pier that strode on shivery legs into a sea of gunmetal silk-edged with flounces of creamy lace, like the expensive lingerie she had loved once. Now she was glad of her thermal vest and her hair blew about her head as brittle and dry as the wind-bitten tamarisk and southernwood bushes.

Hotel gossip had it that Miss Fitzgerald, despite her rags and carrier bags, was very rich. Any discussion of her eccentricities would include, at some point, the refrain, 'She comes of a very good family, you know.' The black sheep driven from some half-ruined Anglo-Irish castle, Miss Agnew surmised, as she hurried along, merging into the wall when Miss Fitzgerald stopped to investigate a litterbin, muttering furiously as discarded newspapers and polystyrene foam cups and boxes showered the pavement. The few people she encountered made wide curves round her, swerving into the road as she marched on with the tail and paws of a long-deceased animal round her neck lashing the wind. Were there sheep in Ireland, Miss Agnew wondered? Pigs and chickens certainly, and grey geese in Kilnevin: perhaps St Patrick had rid the Emerald Isle of sheep with the snakes. She reflected that she was getting sillier and sillier every day that she spent at the Blair Atholl; it was because she had nothing to think about. Perhaps she was manifesting early symptoms of Alzheimer's disease, brought on by the gallons of tea she had poured over the years from the aluminium teapot; aluminium found in quantities in tea, she had read recently, was a contributory factor to the disease, and that friendly familiar teapot, like a battered silver ball reflecting the firelight in the facets of its dented sides, must have made her an almost inevitable candidate for premature senility. Why else would she be following Miss Fitzgerald's erratic and litter-strewn progress, playing detective in the icy wind? The teapot had belonged to Pat, the friend she had lived with for thirty-three years. The lease of the flat had been in Pat's name too, and when it had expired Miss Agnew had neither the means nor the desire to renew it. She hoped that Pat was not watching now, and feeling that her friend's purposeless life negated the years they had spent together, but the brightness and laughter and strength that had been Pat was a heap of ash in a plastic urn, so of course she couldn't see her.

Miss Fitzgerald struck up a side road and Miss Agnew followed her past the guest houses with hanging baskets and gnomes and cards in the windows advertising vacancies, whose names, the Glens and the Blairs and the Lochs and the Braes, suggested that they were passing through a settlement of Scots in exile. They emerged into the long road called Seaside and Miss Agnew found herself studying a green plaster rabbit and a set of ruby-red plastic tumblers on the deck of a broken radiogram in the window of a junk shop, while Miss Fitzgerald contracted some business with its proprietor. A sign stuck to the glass said: 'Lloyd Loom Chairs Wanted Any Condition. Good Prices Paid.' How odd, thought Miss Agnew, that those prosaic wicker chairs should have become collector's items; if you waited long enough everything came back into fashion, but she knew that she would not. Not yet antique, and certainly unfashionable, she stepped into an adjacent shop doorway as Miss Fitzgerald emerged still talking volubly and stuffing something into one of her plastic carriers. Miss Agnew remembered that there was a creaking circle of green wicker chairs in the Blair Atholl conservatory, which she felt suddenly sure were genuine Lloyd Looms. Miss Fitzgerald crossed the road and stood at the bus stop, but Miss Agnew decided to walk on a little before retreating to the Blair Atholl, although a heavy shower had started to fall.

This part of town seemed to be called Roselands; there was a men's club of that name, and a café: the name shimmered softly in tremulous green leaves and pink blowzy petals, the name of a ballroom or dance hall in a film, where the lost and lonely waltzed away their afternoons, reflected in mirrors full of echoes and regret.

Miss Agnew opted for the Rosie Lee Café, which seemed cheerful and steamy, where memory would not draw up a chair at her table and sit down, but as she pushed open the door she saw a fellow resident of the Blair Atholl, Mr Cable, a redundant bachelor late of the now-defunct Bird's Eye factory, seated there smoothing out the creases from a very black-looking newspaper prior to applying himself to the Quiz-word. She retreated. The shower had spent itself now. All the bright and garish gardens she passed, the tubs and window boxes of the terraced houses, and the flowers in the interstices of the paving stones, the shining windows and letter boxes had a desperate air, as if neatness could stave off desolation; a cold salt wind was blowing off the sea and a palm tree rattled behind a closed gate. Tall pampas grass was lashing the houses with canes, softening the blows with hanks of dirty candy-floss, and punishing again. There was too much sky in Eastbourne, Miss Agnew thought, she found its pearly vastness terrifying; gold light poured from the Downs gilding bleakly the cold glass panes of a Victorian red-brick church and blazing in puddles on the road and pavement. Mothers with prams and pushchairs on their way to collect older children from school seemed unaware of, or immune to, all this gold that rolled from the spokes of their wheels, drenched them and turned their baby carriages to chariots of gold.

Miss Agnew had to pause to snatch her breath back from the wind outside a low building set back from the pavements; it was a newly refurbished home for the terminally old. A large yellow van with 'Sleepeezee' on its side was parked in the drive and a mattress was being carried in. Behind a window Miss Agnew saw a girl in a white uniform bounce up towards the ceiling and as she came down a young man bounced up. Up and down they went, trampolining, bounce up, bounce down, laughing, until for a second they were in mid-air in each other's arms before tumbling down in an embrace on the new mattress; the living were larking about on the deathbeds.

Miss Agnew was at once elated and distressed. An image came into her mind of her parents, long ago tucked up in their marble double bed with a quilt of green marble chippings to keep them warm. She caught a bus back to the town centre, and as she sat on its upper deck, she decided that it was right that the young should embrace in the face of death, and closed her ears to the profanities of a bunch of smoking schoolchildren sprawling about the back of the bus; their harsh cries sounded as sad as the voices of sea birds on a deserted beach at dusk.

As she stepped out of the lift on the fourth floor she noticed a pram, belonging to one of the bed-and-breakfast families, wedged across the narrow stair that led to their quarters, and saw the disappearing draggled hem of a sari above a pair of men's socks. She shook the raindrops from her mac and hung it up and made herself a cup of soup and a piece of toast. Later that evening she went down to the conservatory to watch the nine o'clock news.

'Pull the door to, would you?' said Mrs MacConochie. 'There's a draught.' The wind was buffeting the glass panes, the television picture shivered.

'I don't want to be part of this,' Miss Agnew said to herself, looking round, at the Crosbie twins counting stitches, the defeated fan of playing cards in Mrs MacConochie's hand, Mr Cable clawing his winnings, a pile of one-pence pieces, across the baize table whose legs were criss-crossed with black insulating tape. Wicker creaked under old bones, the horizontal hold slipped and Miss Fitzgerald mumbled under a cashmere shawl. 'I don't want to be a drinker of Cup-A-soup in a decaying hotel room, whose only post is a catalogue for thermal underwear,' thought Miss Agnew, 'just as I do not want to joint the respectable army of pensioners in their regimental issue beige and aqua raincoats, whose hair is teased, at a reduced rate on Wednesdays, into white sausages that reveal the vulnerable pink scalps beneath, and who are driven to luncheon clubs in church halls by cheerful volunteers. I am not nearly ready to sleep easy on a Sleepeezee mattress. Something's got to happen.'

The weather forecast ended.

'Have you put on your stove?' Mrs MacConochie asked Mr Cable. He had. It was Mrs MacConochie's colonial past that made her thus refer to the dangerous little electric circles with flayed flexes that failed to heat the residents' rooms; her own room was almost filled by a Benares brass table with folding beaded legs, and burnished peacocks with coloured inlaid tails, and a parade of black elephants with broken tusks; herds of such elephants trumpeted silently in the junk shops and jumble sales of Eastbourne.

The Albanian paused outside the conservatory, then stuck her head round the door.

'Good evening everybody.'

There was a murmur at this diversion; they glimpsed tangerine chiffon and a dusting of glitter on the blue-black plumes of her hair. She smiled, like a dutiful daughter, round the circle of her surrogate family, but there was nobody there to tell her to take care and not to be home late, and she melted away into the mysterious night.

'Pull the door to, would you?' called Mrs MacConochie, wrapping her tartan rug tighter round her knees. 'There's a draught.'

'Something must happen,' said Miss Agnew to herself again as she prepared herself for bed. 'Something will change.'

In the morning nothing had changed. A seagull laughed long and bitterly outside her window. Mr Metalious still disliked her; there was nothing in her pigeon-hole. A grey rain was slashing the street. As she crossed the foyer she passed the Albanian, a poor broken moth caught by the morning, dragging dripping wings of tangerine gauze across the dusty carpet, blue-jawed and sooty-eyed in the fluorescent light.

The only thing that was different, she noticed as she entered the conservatory, was that all the Lloyd Loom chairs had gone, and Miss Fitzgerald was standing under a paper parasol in the rain, watching a van pull away from the back entrance of the hotel.

A CASE OF KNIVES

Candia McWilliam

Lucas Salik, eminent surgeon, is accustomed to performing bold experiments upon other people's hearts. Many might think him a cold-hearted man. But Lucas is obsessed with Hal Darbo and he can see his tenuous hold on him slipping away with Hal's intention to marry.

Together with his friend and confidante, Anne Cowdenbeath, Lucas embarks on an experiment odder than any that takes place in his hospital. His subject is Cora, a young girl conveniently without family ties – and ripe for emotional vivisection. But blood sports can be dangerous and opposition to them fanatical. Sinister happenings begin to disrupt the tidy plan . . .

'This writing is so extraordinary that I am tempted to call it an opera. It is a high and extravagant style, voluptuous, avid and epigrammatic, passionate and risky'
Sunday Telegraph

'Candia McWilliam is artful. *A Case of Knives* is elegant and really quite savage . . . I welcome this natural successor to Iris Murdoch'
Punch

'Poised, startling and innovative . . . an astonishingly accomplished writer'
Anita Brookner

'. . . very fresh, very sharp, and as memorable as a nightmare. It is a brilliant and distinguished book. I was astounded by it'
Peter Levi

Joint winner of the Betty Trask Award and shortlisted for the Whitbread Best Novel Prize

GOOD BEHAVIOUR

Molly Keane

'I do know how to behave – believe me, because I know. I have always known . . .'

Behind the gates of Temple Alice the aristocratic Anglo-Irish St Charles family sinks into a state of decaying grace. To Aroon St Charles, large and unlovely daughter of the house, the fierce forces of sex, money, jealousy and love seem locked out by the ritual patterns of good behaviour. But crumbling codes of conduct cannot hope to save the members of the St Charles family from their own unruly and inadmissible desires.

This elegant and allusive novel coming after years of silence establishes Molly Keane as the natural successor to Jean Rhys.

'An extraordinary *tour de force* of fictional presentation . . . a masterpiece . . . a technically remarkable work, as sharp as a blade . . . Molly Keane is a mistress of wicked comedy.'
Malcolm Bradbury, *Vogue*

'This self-possessed, crisply detailed and alertly funny novel is a wonder. Silent for decades, Keane has abruptly produced a masterpiece.'
Newsweek

'A witty, black comedy of manners, *Good Behaviour* is a memorable novel by an Irish writer whose only equal is Elizabeth Bowen.'
The Bookseller

'May well become a classic among English novels.'
Rachel Billington, *New York Times Book Review*

'Fine new novel, wickedly alive.'
Victoria Glendinning, *Sunday Times*

'Enchanting.'
Edna O'Brien, *Observer*

HEAT AND DUST

Ruth Prawer Jhabvala

The beautiful, spoiled, and bored Olivia, married to a civil servant, outrages society in the tiny, suffocating Indian town of Satipur by eloping with an Indian prince. This is her story and that of her step-granddaughter who, fifty years later, goes back to the heat, the dust and the squalor of the bazaars to solve the enigma of Olivia's scandal.

'A superb book. A complex story line, handled with dazzling assurance ... moving and profound. Ruth Prawer Jhabvala has not only written a love story, she has also exposed the soul and nerve ends of a fascinating and compelling country. This is a book of cool, controlled brilliance. It is a jewel to be treasured.'
The Times

THE SUMMER AFTER THE FUNERAL

Jane Gardam

A rather mysterious old clergyman is dead, and his most adoring child, sixteen-year-old Athene, is desolate. A statuesque beauty, greatly admired, she is also lonely, untouchable and living a secret life of fairly dangerous fantasy.

Athene's mother, at once highly organised and monumentally vague, dispatches her children to spend the holidays with assorted friends and relatives. For Athene, victim of plans gone awry, that golden summer after the funeral becomes deliciously puzzling fodder for her fantasy. Stuck in a seaside hotel with an inarticulate and beautiful boy, marooned in a seaside cottage with a painter, and finally alone in an empty school with a young master, she finds that men are not all as saintly as her father – and that she is far from saintly herself . . .

'The pattern of *The Summer After the Funeral*, like that of an Iris Murdoch satire, is as intricate and delicate as a mazurka . . . To enjoy the full impact of this marvellously entertaining book one cannot afford to skip a single word'
TLS

'Extraordinary . . . Mrs Gardam is a writer of original spirit, her observations acute and funny/sad'
The Guardian

'Jane Gardam to me is everything that's right about contemporary fiction . . . there's nothing more difficult than trying to catch a mood, and I think she does that to perfection'
Margaret Forster

Jane Gardam's *The Queen of the Tambourine* is the winner of the 1991 Whitbread Best Novel of the Year Award

ABACUS